THE KEEPER

THE KEEPER

GUADALUPE GARCÍA McCALL

HARPER

An Imprint of HarperCollinsPublishers

Library of Congress Control Number: 2021943909
ISBN 978-0-06-307692-1

Typography by Catherine Lee
21 22 23 24 25 GV 10 9 8 7 6 5 4 3 2 1
❖
First Edition

To Julie, always remember your Ita loves you!

THE KEEPER

CHAPTER 1

The darkness comes upon us so quickly, I just know it's a sign. This move across the country to Brentville, Oregon, is all wrong for us. I can feel it, deep down in the pit of my stomach—leaving Texas was a big mistake. Selling our little house in Somerset was a mistake too, because now we don't have a place to go back to. But the biggest mistake was moving all the way up here, to a state known for having the largest fungus in America. Honestly, who brags about that? Not that I could've stopped any of it. I'm only twelve years old. Wherever my parents go, I have to go with them, fungus or no fungus.

"It's going to rain," I say, peering up at the darkening sky. "It always rains out here, you know. We'll be wet and miserable for the rest of our lives."

"Actually, it rains less than half the year out here, James." My father parks the car in our new driveway and gets out. He puts his hands on his waist and stretches, arching his back and twisting his neck.

"It rains one hundred and sixty days a year out here, which might as well be all the time. That's 43.8 percent of the time. I know. I looked it up," I say as I open the car door to get out.

"Careful not to let your chucho out," my mother says. "Not without his leash. He doesn't know the neighborhood."

I push on Baxter's chest gently and give his thick black fur a friendly tug. "Stay with Ava," I tell him.

But Baxter whines and looks over at my little sister, Ava, whose slack face is pressed against the window on the other side of the car. It's been a while since he went number one, at least two hours, and I can see he needs to come out.

"Oh, okay," I say as I look around for his leash on the floorboard. Finding it, I clip it to his collar and let him climb out of the car. I walk around with him, letting him find a good place to lift his leg. Baxter does his business against a stump far from the house, on the edge of the property, before we walk over to my parents on the other side of the yard.

"Now, there's a grand view if I ever saw one!" my father says, and my mother grins as she leans into him.

My mother puts her hand to her forehead to shade her eyes and takes a deep breath. "I've never seen so many trees in my life! They're so . . . majestic."

I take my phone out of my pocket and try to turn it on, but it's no use. It's dead.

"It's impressive," my father tells my mother.

I'm not impressed. To be honest, I am feeling a little caged in—missing the brightness of summers in Texas. This wall of trees goes on forever, surrounding us, closing us in. The dark-gray sliver of sky above promises to make everything cold and dismal. And because it's been raining here, the air is an invisible moist mist that won't let me breathe.

I want to complain, to say for the billionth time how much I want to go back home. But I know that no matter what I say, it's all going to fall on deaf ears, because my mother is in love with this place. She hasn't stopped showing us pictures of it since my parents made the decision to take new jobs and move us out here.

That's three months of long family discussions about "making sacrifices to get ahead in life." Three months of oohs and ahhs over everything Oregon. Three months of *Look at these Douglas firs. Christmas trees, everywhere! We can go see the migrating whales. And, oh, there's a cave with sea lions. Don't you want to explore the Columbia River Gorge?*

Standing in the side yard, my mother takes a deep breath, smiles, and says, "Mother Nature really outdid herself up here."

In the back seat, Ava stirs and wakes up. She lumbers out of the car, rubbing her eyes and yawning. She walks over, reaches out, and takes Baxter's leash out of my hand.

"Give him to me," she says. "He's my dog!" And she walks behind Baxter, who's eager to explore the rest of the yard with her. Ava is ten now. She's very independent, so she doesn't always let me help her. And since Baxter hasn't gone number two yet,

I'm happy to let her take care of that.

"What is it, boy? What did you find?" Ava leans over to look at whatever Baxter is sniffing at. Then she pulls a very large, moldy-looking mushroom out of the ground. "Whoa! Look at this!"

"What are you doing?" I ask, horrified, because Ava is waving the huge gray toadstool in my face.

"Eat it!" she says, laughing. "Eat it! Eat it!"

"Give me that!" I tell her, reaching up to take the giant fungus out of her hands. "Why do you always have to touch everything?"

But instead of letting me have it, Ava swipes the disgusting mushroom away and takes off with it. "No, it's mine!" she giggles, and runs away with Baxter loping beside her.

I run after them, catch up to her, and knock the monstrous thing out of her hand. Ava stops and tosses the broken stem beside its broken hood. I pick up the nasty pieces of mushroom, walk up to the tree line to the left of the house, and toss them into the dark woods.

"Why'd you do that?" Pulling Baxter along, Ava walks over to me at the tree line. "I was gonna study that under my microscope!"

While Ava walks Baxter up to the porch, our parents stand side by side in the front yard, happy as holly berries, holding hands and taking in the sight of our new house.

"Look at what we did, Chris." My mother slips her arms around my father's waist and stands on tiptoe to plant a kiss on his chin. "We did this. You and me. Together."

My father smiles smugly. "Yup. We've come a long way for two kids from the border," he says.

"Yes, we have." My mother nods. "We're blessed."

Blessed?

I can see why they think that. This towering house with its tall stained-glass windows and fancy architecture is my mother's dreams coming true. I guess in her eyes they have because we moved here for her new job. Up here, in Oregon, my mother is Assistant Professor Marina Ruiz-McNichols—the first girl from her small town of Eagle Pass to ever get a PhD and teach at a big-time university.

My father's a computer analyst, and he can always find a good job. That's why it was so easy for my parents to—like my Ita, my maternal grandmother, used to say—pick up our tiliches and move everybody's personal stuff all the way out here.

I don't want to be mad about it, but I am.

"Come on," my father says, waving us over. "Let's go check out the house."

In the living room, the fireplace crackles and snaps, releasing a scent that makes the house smell like ashes mixed in with some kind of flower-scented candle. Ava lets Baxter loose, and he goes around sniffing the wooden floorboards before he walks over and plants himself in front of the hearth. He puts his head down over his front paws and stares at the glowing embers.

"Will you look at that! Mrs. Benson must have sent someone over to start a fire for us," my mother says. "She's the best real estate agent ever. I'm going to have to do something nice for her later."

"Because that's not creepy at all, having some stranger let themselves into our house when we're not here," I whisper to Ava. But she covers her ears and turns her face away from me.

"James Anthony McNichols! Stop trying to scare your sister!" My mother's brows knit themselves over her eyes like two angry caterpillars. I want to tell her that her face is going to get stuck like that, but I don't.

Ava rubs her hands over the crackling embers. "I like it. It makes the house smell like . . . like . . ."

"Burning flesh?" I whisper, finishing Ava's thought with my best devilish grin.

"I was going to say *spring*." Ava punctuates the word *spring* with air quotes.

I inhale too deeply, and the flowery scent gets caught in the back of my throat. I cough, covering my mouth with my shirt. "Whoa, that's strong."

"I like the smell," my mother says. "It's soothing." Then she strolls around the living room, putting her hands on everything she sees. "I love it all—the sparkling chandelier, the vaulted ceiling, the wooden railing. Of course, the circular stairway is my absolute favorite."

My father sits on a stool at the breakfast bar and swivels around to us. "It's a beautiful house. It's way more spacious than I thought it would be."

"I know!" my mother squeals. She puts her arms around my father's back and presses a loud kiss on his blond head, right behind his ear. "Most houses look so big in the pictures, then you get there, and they're tighter than you expected. But not this one."

"Nope." My father kisses and pats my mother's hand. "This one doesn't disappoint. I can tell already—we're going to be very happy here."

I stare at the fireplace and sigh. Baxter stares up at me, and I cover my nose with my shirt again.

"This is so exciting!" Ava says, and she runs up the circular stairway like a cochinilla, a tiny pill bug rounding the stairs in a hurry, before she disappears.

"What about you, James?" my father asks. "Aren't you excited? How lucky are we, huh?"

"Pretty lucky," I say, holding my shirt over my mouth and nose at the far end of the living room.

Ava comes running down the stairs. "I get the room with the big window!" she yells as she jumps off the last step.

"Uh-uh," I say. "I'm the oldest. I get first dibs."

Ava shakes her head. "Nope. Only the best for the youngest."

"Ava, you know that's not true," my father says. "Why don't you two flip for it? Come over here. You can call it, if you want."

Ava grins at me as she crosses the room to try out her luck. She stands next to my father at the counter. "Heads. I call heads," she says, when my father pulls out a quarter and puts it over his thumb.

"Is tails okay with you, James?" my father asks.

I shrug.

"Whatever," I say because, honestly, nothing here is ever going to be all right. With or without a big window in my room, I'll still be in Oregon. So, I watch my father toss the coin high up in the air, where it flips and glints before he catches it in midair. Then he slaps it down on the back of his hand.

"Tails!" my father calls and smiles over at me.

"Awww . . ." Ava's shoulders sag, and she looks up at our father and pleads. "Let's go again. Best two out of three."

I roll my eyes.

"No," my father says, pinching her nose. "Your brother won it, fair and square."

"Are you okay, Jaimito?" my mother asks me. "What's the matter? You don't like the house?"

Hearing her call me by my Spanish name, *Jaimito*, makes me cringe. It's the only name my Ita ever called me. It hurts to have my mother use it like this, while she's trying to sell me on this house—this new start.

But today is not the time to tell her that. Ita's only been gone for a month and a half. Forty-four days. I know, I've been counting, waiting for the day we can talk about my Ita without feeling sad that she didn't get to make the trip with us, like she would have if she hadn't gotten so sick.

I give my mother a thumbs-up and grin under my shirt, which is still pulled up over my nose. She comes over and touches my forehead. "What's going on with you? Are you playing sick?" she asks. "I'm not buying it, little imp. I know your tricks."

I sigh heavily, because I wish I could make her understand just how doomed this whole move feels. "This house smells like a crem—crema—cremetery!" I say, stumbling to find the right word. "It stinks like a cremetery in here!"

"You mean crematory, or crematorium, either is correct," my father says. "But that's not very nice. It's inappropriate to talk like that."

My mother unmasks me.

"You need to stop," she tells me. "You promised to give this move a chance!"

My mother puts her hands on my cheeks and tilts up my head. Her warm brown eyes check my face. When she gets closer, I stick out my tongue and lick my lips quickly, like a salamander.

She makes a startled noise and then laughs at herself. "Oh, you're such a silly lagartijo!"

"He'll be all right," my father says, chuckling from across the room. "He just needs to acclimate. But he's a good little lizard. He'll feel better once we get some food into him. How does pizza sound? Pepperoni? Mom? Ava? Medium cheese for James?"

"Nope," my mother says. "There's no pizza delivery. Not all the way out here."

"No delivery?" I frown at my father. "What kind of place is this?"

"A gated community. Very posh." My father winks.

"But very secluded," my mother chimes in. "Never fear, Mrs.

Benson said she stocked the fridge!" My mother holds the refrigerator door open and steps aside so we can see that every shelf is full of goodies.

"Well, she just became my favorite neighbor," my father says.

Someone knocks on the door—an unexpected rapping that startles us all. My father gets up. "I'll get it."

"Mrs. Benson!" my mother says, when a plump, white-haired woman slips through the front door holding a huge plate of cookies in her hands.

"I see Henry got the fire going." Mrs. Benson smiles smugly. Her thin lips pull at her cheeks and crinkle at the corners of her bright gray eyes. "I knew it was going to rain, so I sent Henry up here to take care of it for you."

"Thank you so much for the groceries," my father says, closing the door to keep out the draft. "You didn't have to do that."

"Yes. Thank you," my mother says. "For everything."

"Oh, it was our pleasure. Henry and I wanted to make sure you feel welcome in our neighborhood," Mrs. Benson says. "It's important."

My mother smiles. "Are those for us?" she asks.

Mrs. Benson looks from me to Ava. Her smile is a little tight-lipped. She tries to hand Ava the plate of cookies, but Ava looks up at my mother as if waiting for approval. My mother takes the cookies, and Mrs. Benson walks toward me. As she gets closer, I can see her better. Her gray-white hair is brittle as straw, and when she leans over I see that she's very wrinkly. She looks a little nervous, like she's trying hard to make a good impression but doesn't quite know what to do or say.

"Is this *your young man James?*" Mrs. Benson extends her hand to me. I'm sure it's not her fault, but her old lady's breath is a little sour, so I pull the collar of my shirt up over my mouth and nose again.

"James?" my father says. "Don't be rude. Shake the lady's hand."

I let my shirt go and shake the old woman's hand. "Thanks for the cookies," I say. "I'm sure they're delicious."

Mrs. Benson's smile widens. Her gray eyes sparkle down at me, and she suddenly looks like that cartoon of Mrs. Claus that plays on TV every year.

"Welcome, James. Welcome." Mrs. Benson pats my hand. Then she lets me go and turns to look at my mother again. "I can't wait for everyone to meet you and your beautiful children."

"Everyone?" I ask. "Who's everyone?"

"The community," Mrs. Benson explains. "There's Mr. Brent. He lives down the street, and Mr. and Mrs. Harvey live around the bend. Mr. Morris and his daughter, Betty, are just up the road, over the hill. This street is a circle, so including Ms. Phillips, the Johnsons, Mrs. Coleman, and the Martins, we all live on the same road. But the village is much, much bigger. There are twenty-five streets altogether, with all kinds of families, large and small."

"Really?" my mother asks. "I didn't realize we had so many neighbors."

"Oh, yes." Mrs. Benson smiles. Her lips form a tight little line

11

that she presses together. "We're a very close-knit community. But don't worry about trying to figure out who's who. You'll meet them all at the meet and greet this weekend."

"Meet and greet?" my mother asks.

"Yes, the community voted," she says. "We're having a cook-out. Oh, don't worry. It's nothing fancy. Just a little barbecue. Out here in the quad. In your honor."

"Oh, that sounds great," my father says. "I'll put it on the calendar."

Beside my mother, my sister is lifting the plastic wrap off the plate of cookies.

"Ooooooh!" Ava says, as she eyes the huge chocolate chip chunks on the thick cookies.

"Not before you wash your hands," my mother says. "You touched that dirty mushroom out there. Go on."

"I have to clean up too," I say, and I run off behind Ava.

While I wait for Ava to wash her hands, I peek into the bedrooms. "Good job on the coin toss," I tease her. "Big window's nice."

"Don't gloat," she says, frowning as she walks downstairs.

Later, after a dinner of fish tacos and a quick video game battle in our new living room, I go up to my room. I can't call my best friends, Beto and Mike, because I put the leftover honey from my road biscuit on Ava's face while she was sleeping in the car. Baxter went nuts trying to lick her face off, and my mother took my phone away. She said I was distracting my father's driving, but I think they were just cranky. Four days on the road will do that to parents.

Instead of talking to friends, I pick up my Knight Owl, the monocular telescope I got for my tenth birthday. So far, it's the best present I've ever received. Well, maybe not the best. I like my phone too. But I use this scope to look at everything from stars in the sky to wildlife at night, because it has night vision.

I put the scope around my neck and sneak out of my room through the window to lie on the small roof of the porch. Lying back, I use the Stargazer mode to look up at the Oregon night sky. I know it's the same constellations, the same galaxies, the same universe I'm living in, but I can't help it. Without my friends to play with and without my Ita to tell us fanciful stories at night, I feel a little lost in this part of the world.

I don't know why I am such a pain to my parents, but I know I need to find a better way of letting them know how I feel. Because, although there's really nothing wrong with this new place, I don't belong here.

But how do I convince them this isn't the best place for all of us, when my parents think that, here, we have it all? A beautiful new house. A majestic forest. Welcoming people. Community.

Why would my parents ever move back home? It's not like anyone is waiting for them back there. My father has no more family there, and my Ita was the only family my mother had left. And now that she's gone . . .

It hits me then—and I sit straight up. Oh my God!

We're *never* going back to Texas!

CHAPTER 2

I wake up the next morning with a new goal in mind. I'm going to be a good son. Even if I'm not happy about leaving my two best friends, Beto and Mike, back in Texas, I decide to pretend that I'm okay for a while. Because the sooner I can convince my parents that everything's all right, the sooner I can get my phone back. Then I can text with Beto and Mike and listen to my Ita's "Kooky Cuentos" or "Consejos From the Other Side"—the two collections of videos I recorded on my phone, before she passed away.

It's the only thing I have left of her.

"What do you want?" Ava asks when I stand outside her bedroom door and Baxter rushes over to lick my hand.

"Why do I have to want something to come over?" I ask. "I just wanted to check out your room."

"Yeah, well, it doesn't have a big window, does it?" she asks. Then she lifts her arm and makes a long, sweeping gesture over

14

to the single-pane window with its view of the street because her room is at the front of the house.

"But you've got Baxter," I say. She's such a sore loser. It's kind of annoying, since it's not like my parents ignore or neglect her. She has a lot of things I don't have. "I never got a dog for my birthday. He's all yours."

When he hears his name, Baxter jumps up, puts his paws on my chest, and licks my chin. I pull back so he can't reach my mouth. Doggy kisses are so gross if you don't close your mouth.

Ava shakes her head as she plops two more dolls on the mountain of muñecas sitting on her dresser. "Yeah, I can feel the love all the way over here."

"What?" I ask, petting Baxter's dark head, because he's really a great dog. He's loving and loyal and, even though he's technically Ava's dog, he follows me around everywhere I go. "I'm not doing anything. I never have."

"Seriously? You put little bags with bacon bits in your pockets for months when we first got him," Ava accuses. "That's why he loves you so much. He remembers the bacon."

"I'm sorry," I say, because she's never going to believe me that I used the bacon to house-train him. But the proof is right here, in front of her. Baxter's never had an accident inside the house, not since he was a pup. "I wasn't trying to take him away from you. Promise."

Ava huffs.

"Just go!" she says, and she turns back to unpacking the rest

15

of her muñecas. She takes her lasso, the long rope my parents gave her when she became fascinated with the San Antonio Rodeo, and puts it on her rocking chair. Then she pulls out her microscope and sets it on her desk, next to her stack of petri dishes. "And close the door. I don't want to be bothered while I'm decorating."

"Can Baxter come with me? I'm going to throw the ball outside," I say, and when she frowns at me, I add, "You can come too. We can play fetch with him."

"No," she says. "He's helping me fix my room. Now leave us alone. And close the door behind you."

Because I know my sister, I know she's not ready to let go of this dumb grudge. Arguing with her is pointless right now, so I reach in and pull the door shut before I head down the hall, carrying my mixed emotions with me as I go, like a giant sack of potatoes. On the one hand, I'm annoyed that Ava can't just get over losing; on the other, I'm kind of scared of what life is going to be like in Oregon if even my sister isn't talking to me.

"James?" my mother calls as I walk past her new home office at the top of the stairs.

I stop and take a few steps backward, so that I am in her line of vision. I even raise my eyebrows, trying to look super interested in whatever my mother is about to ask of me, even though I hate chores and she knows it.

"Yes?"

"Can you help me put things up in here?" she asks, making

ojitos, those loving little eyes she puts on every time she wants me to join her on the dark side—*the joy of organizing!*

Reminding myself that I need to get my phone back, I paste a smile on my face and say, "Sure. What'd you need?"

"I want to put my Nahua artifacts up today," she says, looking into a box. "Not all of them. Some of them will go in my new office on campus, but I'd like to put most things up in here."

"Okay," I say, looking around at all the empty shelves and blank walls. "Just tell me what goes where."

We take our time unpacking, carefully unrolling the bubble wrap away from each piece, and placing each item on the shelves and desk. There are so many things: small statues of gods and goddesses, a heavy stone bowl with a carving of a serpent, a sharp black knife, and some framed prints—drawings and photographs.

"What's this doing in here?" I ask as I pull out a picture of my Ita.

"Awww! There she is!" my mom exclaims. Her voice is a soft sigh. But when she reaches over and takes the picture from me, I don't let it go right away.

Looking at my Ita staring back at me from behind the glass reminds me of all the silly stories she used to tell us. Her own special take on old fairy tales, stories like "Moldy Muñecas" and "Crafty Cucarachas," always made me and Ava laugh. Nobody could tell a scary story like my Ita, with her tales of monsters and ghouls from the Rio Grande. Nobody could bring La Llorona's horrific wail to life the way she did. But her consejos, the *wise words* Ita wanted me to record on my phone when I visited her at the hospital after school, are special. She said they would help me and Ava stay connected to her for always. It's too bad Ava can't watch any of the videos yet, because even the kooky tales make her cry her eyes out.

"Oh, I'm sorry," my mother says. "Did you want to put it up?"

"No. It's okay," I say, releasing the picture.

"What do you think?" she asks, pulling the flap behind it open and placing it gently on the shelf above her desktop, next to one of the creepiest things in my mother's office.

I scan the drawing and read the label.

"Tlātlāhuihpochtin, the Luminous Ones." I look closely at their creepy forms and frown. "Is this really where you want it? Shouldn't we put it somewhere else in the house, like on the mantel over the fireplace?"

Instead of agreeing with me, my mother smiles, leans over, and moves the picture so that the two frames are closer to each other. "No," she says. "This is where she belongs now. With the antepasados, our beloved ancestors."

"Really?" I ask, looking at the drawing of strange winged creatures—vampiric vultures and buzzards and owls in flight. "Weren't these people cursed? Didn't they have to eat children or something?"

"Only the bad ones."

When I raise my eyebrows, my mother laughs. She reaches

over, pulls me in for a hug, and squeezes me tight, giving me a flurry of those loud, hard-pressed kisses she loves to give, until I can't take it anymore and I wiggle out of her embrace.

"Okay," I say. "That's enough love for today."

"What's the matter?" my mother asks, letting me go and watching me sort through the last few items in the box on her desk.

Though my mother's not saying it outright, her teasing tells me she thinks I'm a brat. It's true that I haven't been the best-behaved kid lately. I admit, I was acting up a lot before we moved, but I just wish she could see that deep down I'm really a good kid. I don't get in trouble at school, and I make really good grades and, regardless of what it might look like, I do love my little sister. Even though she is super annoying and deserves every single prank I've ever played on her.

"I'm sorry I've been such a pain lately, complaining and playing pranks on Ava all the time," I tell her. "I would never hurt her, you know."

"Oh, I know it's not all one-sided," my mother says, shifting my Ita's picture so that it's facing the window. "Ava gives as good as she gets. I just want the two of you to find your footing in this new place."

"I know," I say. "It's just hard, that's all. Moving all the way out here. I'm not sure we'll fit in. What if people don't—like us? What if moving away was a mistake?"

My mother sits down in her wingback chair and pulls me

19

down so that we are sitting side by side, looking out the window at the sunny day yesterday's rain left behind. "Life is an adventure, Jaimito. We aren't meant to stay cooped up in one place, in one house, in one town, all the time."

I look out the window. Ava is out in the backyard now, picking specimens, weeds and wildflowers she stuffs into a baggie while Baxter pulls on his leash behind her.

"Maybe you should go outside," my mother says. "Spend some time with your sister."

"She's not talking to me," I tell her. "She thinks I'm trying to steal her dog."

"Aww, come on." My mother laughs and hugs me, pulling me closer, even though I am too old to sit on her lap. "That's not true. Ava loves you."

"Oh, it shows," I say sarcastically, and I look at my sister laughing at Baxter as she chases him around in the yard.

"What?" my mother asks. "Where is this coming from?"

"Well, I tried being nice earlier, but she threw me out of her room."

My mother ruffles my hair. "You know, it's not just about her. This relationship is also about you."

I wiggle around until she lets me go and I can stand up again. "I don't mean to be a bad brother," I tell her. "She's just so annoying sometimes!"

My mother sighs. "Well, like anything else, I think this is going to take practice. You're just going to have to practice being a good brother."

"Practice? This isn't baseball, Mom," I complain.

"Oh, you can do this." My mother gets up and peers out the window. "Look at her. She's bored. What would she do if she didn't have you?"

"Celebrate," I say, sighing.

My mother puts her hands on my shoulders and guides me to stand directly in front of the window. "Go on. Get out there. Play nice with your sister. And no more pranks. You promised."

I look at my sister, who's holding a tiny flower in her hand as she stares out at the dark, deep woods with Baxter sitting by her side. "I'm going to need my phone back," I tell my mother. "In case of an emergency. Like if she goes hog wild on me and wants to take off to collect specimens. You know how she gets."

"I do." My mother laughs. "She's very curious. But that's part of the package—just the way God intended her to be. And we love her for it."

"I guess," I say, because Ava can be stubborn, and difficult, and just plain bossy sometimes, but she's also gifted. She's smart in ways I will never be smart, which is kind of frustrating, because I have to work hard to get good grades. I'm not saying I'm jealous or anything. It's just something else I have to deal with every day, trying to keep up with her. "So, can I have my phone back?"

My mother grins. "Well . . . that's your father's department."

When I get outside, Ava pretends that I don't exist.

"Wanna throw the ball?" I ask her.

Ava shakes her head. I look back at our house, at the three-car garage, and think about the fact that we only have two vehicles, so that extra space is holding the things we can't keep inside the house.

"What about the bikes?" I ask, remembering that Dad put our bikes in that third space. "Wanna take a ride around the neighborhood."

"No," Ava says. "I don't want Baxter to feel left behind."

"That makes sense," I say. "It's gonna take time, getting him used to living here, in a new place with new streets."

Ava nods. "New sounds. New smells. New things to bark at," she says.

"Well, I'm sure you can help him get used to it," I tell her.

Ava looks down at the leash in her hand, and I sigh and turn away, because there's no use. She's not ready to get along. "You want to walk Baxter with me?" she asks.

"I was about to ask you that," I say as I spin around to face her. She smiles and nods. "No pranks, though," I warn as we start down the driveway. "I promised Mom we'd stay out of trouble."

"Well, that's convenient!" Ava moans as she turns left and takes to the sidewalk, following Baxter's lead.

"What do you mean?" I ask.

"You want to stop now? After you got the last laugh?" Ava asks. "I don't think so. Besides, I have a really good one coming up."

"Oh, yeah?" I ask her, surprised. Because for a moment back there, it felt like we might be calling a truce. "What were you gonna do?"

"*Am*—what *am* I going to do?" Ava grins her most malcriada grin as she lets Baxter lead us across the street.

"But I promised Mom I wouldn't be doing that out here." I don't mean to whine, it just comes out that way, so I clear my throat and continue. "You promised to behave too. Remember?"

Ava tosses her braid off her shoulder and starts walking faster. "That's okay. I'm saving it up, anyway."

"Saving it up?" I ask.

"For when you least expect it," Ava says. "But it's a *good one*."

"Great . . . I can't wait to get in trouble again," I mumble to myself as we head down the gentle slope on Pine Circle, because there's no way I'm going to let her win, to become the Ultimate Prankmaster, if she pulls a good one out here. That's the thing about prank wars—unless both parties agree, there's no end to them.

When we get to the bottom of the hill, we decide to explore the rest of our neighborhood. We walk down Douglas Fir, turn the corner onto Shortleaf, and walk down Whitebark, and that's when we get a glimpse of them.

Baxter hears them first, and he barks and tugs at his leash, wanting to walk toward the group of kids playing ball at the end of the street, where the pavement ends in a spot far enough away from the tree line to make a kind of natural baseball diamond.

The group of kids doesn't notice us standing there, gawking at them. They're too busy playing. I look around for a coach, but I don't see one. Because there are no adults, I suspect it's some kind of pickup game. Their cheers and laughter are loud enough

23

to make Baxter bark and tug on his leash. Ava's mouth drops open when one of them hits the ball high up in the air where it seems to stand still for a moment before it falls right into the catcher's mitt.

"Baseball!" Ava's eyes sparkle as she looks up at me. "Wanna go play with them?"

Her words bring to mind memories of summer days playing alongside Beto and Mike on Prairie Road. The three of us have been teammates since T-ball. The thought of playing with anyone else, of not having them there to joke with about being able to hit home run after home run every time I get up to the plate, but not catch an easy pop-up, makes my chest hurt.

Would these kids make fun of me, I wonder, *if they knew that I can't catch a fly ball half the time? Would they reject me, tell me to get lost? Or would they work with me, accept me, holey glove and all, the way Beto and Mike always have?*

All of a sudden, I feel like I can't catch my breath, so I look away. Because, frankly, I don't want to find out. Playing with these new kids out here, becoming their teammate, would be like disrespecting the bond Beto, Mike, and I have. Nobody can ever replace them as teammates. We're the Three Amigos—what we had, our friendship, can't be replaced. That's why I told Dad not to look into Little League out here, because I didn't want to play with anyone else. Ever.

Ava nudges me. "Well?"

"Nah. It's just a street game," I tell her. "Besides, I told Dad I'm done with baseball."

Ava looks back at the group of kids. The second batter strikes out. "Are you sure? They could use a good hitter, and you're the best, James."

I look over at her and try to smile, but my lips won't cooperate because, on top of everything else, I can't tell if she's just playing nice or if she really does think I'm that good at baseball.

"I'm sure," I tell her, turning away from the game, because my chest feels like it's going to explode from the pressure building up inside me. "Come on. I wanna check out the rest of the neighborhood."

When we get home, exhausted and ready to eat, my father makes a big announcement. To celebrate our new home, we're having our very first Family Movie Night.

So, while we prepare dinner together, all set up at different stations in our nice big kitchen, we all pitch our movie ideas. While I slice the lettuce and tomatoes for our salad, we settle on watching a horror flick. Mom wants to see *Rebecca,* because it's her favorite horror movie. Dad wants to see *Tarantula!,* but Ava wants to see *The Birds.* And since I have no real horror favorites, it's up to me to vote for which movie we should all watch. Because I really don't care what we watch, I pick Dad's movie. Ava hides her face every time one of the spiders comes onscreen. She doesn't have arachnophobia or anything. But last year she read all about the giant tree spiders in the Amazon jungle, and the tarantulas in the movie are giving her the willies.

Much later, when the movie's over and my father adjusts the sound system so they can't hear us playing video games from their room upstairs, I can't help but think about that game on the street this afternoon.

Maybe I should have gone over there and asked to play with them, I tell myself. *Besides sitting at home with my family, what am I supposed to do for fun in Oregon? I don't have any friends here, and it's not like I can hang out with my little sister for the rest of my life.*

Before we start playing, Ava brings in the tray with hot cocoa she insisted on making without my help. I scoot over on the couch so that she can sit beside Baxter. Ava puts the drink tray down on the coffee table in front of us and passes me the chocolate de olla. I take one of the leftover nutty popcorn treats my mother made for Movie Night.

"Thank you," I say, taking in the delicious scent of my Ita's Mexican cocoa.

Keeping my eyes on the sixty-inch screen, I blow on my drink before taking a big sip. But instead of tasting like my Ita's delicious, cinnamon-chocolately goodness, with extra sugar because that's the way I like it, this tastes like a polluted ocean.

I choke and spit it out quickly, coughing as it all comes out at once.

The hot, dark liquid bursts out of my mouth and goes in a million directions, getting on everything in front of me. My shirt, my pants, the sofa, the carpet, the table, absolutely everything has cocoa-juice-spittle droplets all over it.

"Ava!" I scream.

Beside me, Ava smiles and cringes and makes herself into a small ball on the couch.

"Jaimito!" my mother cries out as she and my father rush down the stairs. "What's wrong? What is it?"

"Is he choking?" My father stands over me. "Are you okay, James?"

Still coughing, I shake my head and point to my cup down on the table. "No—yes—" I say.

"Your drink?" my father asks. "What happened?"

My mother sits next to me and rubs my back. "Did it go down the wrong way?"

"No," I tell them. "It's not cocoa."

My mother frowns. She picks up my cup, sniffs, and looks at my sister.

"Ava—" My mother's voice is a warning that says, *Don't lie to me.*

Ava pulls her pajama collar up, past her neck, and covers her grin with it. "Ooops," she whispers from behind the fabric.

"She put salt in it," I tell my mother. "It tastes like sea muck!"

"Salt!" My mother looks mad.

"I'm sorry," Ava says, grinning as she peeks over at me. "I didn't know he was going to spit it out like that. I'll clean it up."

"You sure will," my mother says. "You know where the cleaning supplies are. Let's go. Get on with it."

"Well, that's it! No more Game Time!" my father says, using the official title for our summertime late-night video games. He looks mad—not flaring-nostrils angry but mad enough that he shuts down the television with a frustrated click and puts away the remote that controls the entertainment systems.

"Thanks a lot," I tell Ava, angry that I didn't see that one coming. I should have known Ava wasn't just trying to be nice by offering to make us something to drink. Frustrated, I use the napkins on the tray to clean myself off as much as I can before I head upstairs.

After showering, I change into my pajamas and sit at my desk to send an email to Mike. I won't tell him about the kids playing that pickup game on the street. I don't want to get into that. I just want to let him know I won't get my phone back until next week.

My father comes into the room to check on me. "You okay?" he asks.

"Yeah," I say, and I let my fingers fall off the keyboard. "Just sending Mike a message. Old-school."

My father's lip twists as he looks at the short message on my screen. "Old-school, huh?" he asks. Then, as if he is reading my mind, he takes my phone out of his pocket and offers it to me.

"Really?" I ask, my voice suddenly high-pitched and squeaky.

"Yes," he says, handing me the phone. "Just take it easy on your sister, okay? Don't retaliate. She's trying to adjust too, you know."

"You could've fooled me," I say. "That prank was well planned."

My father scratches his head and sighs. "She's a worthy adversary," he admits. "But it gets old, you know, this prank war you two have going on, especially when it affects all of us. So, why don't you two just cool it for now?"

I nod and turn on my phone.

My father leans over and kisses my forehead. "Good night, boy."

When he leaves, I lie down in bed and text Beto and Mike on our Three Amigos thread. It's two hours later in Texas, but they're still awake, so they text me back right away. We talk about school for a while, but when they hear what's going on with me, they have a lot to say.

MIKE: dude you can't let her win

you gotta do something

ME: oh don't worry this isn't over yet

she's not getting away with this one

BETO: well if you're gonna get

her back do it right

MIKE: like scare her straight already

BETO: yeah, go big or go home you know

ME: yeah, I know

Half an hour later, I say goodbye and crawl out my window to sit on the porch roof, looking at the stars with my telescope and my phone app. There is something really relaxing about just looking at the stars sitting so close together but knowing that they are really not close at all.

That's how I feel about Ava. We're supposed to be close. She's my sister. And I love her, but when you look at us—really look at us—we couldn't be farther apart if we tried. The truth upsets me, but then, when I think about the mess she made tonight, how she single-handedly destroyed Game Time, just ruined the whole thing for us, I get mad. Nobody should have that much power over their family.

Beto and Mike are right. If I want this prank war to end, I'm going to have to teach her a lesson—a big one.

CHAPTER 3

I stay up till all hours of the night planning my best prank ever and get up extra, extra early to set it up. It isn't easy. I have to be super quiet when I open Ava's door and sneak into her room. I crawl on my hands and knees, and reach up again and again, until I have every single one of her muñecas in my gym bag.

Baxter sleeps at the foot of Ava's bed and wakes up easily, but I am prepared for him. I knew if anything could give me away, it would be him. That's why I taped his noisy tags to the inside of his collar before he and Ava went to bed, so he wouldn't give me away when he moved around. And, except for the flapping of his ears when he shakes his whole body to wake himself up, he doesn't disturb Ava's deep sleep one bit while I *borrow* her precious dolls.

When everything is ready, at 6:55 a.m., I pour myself a bowl of cereal and sit on a stool at the counter to watch the television with the volume off. My father walks in first, followed by my mother, who gives me a quick hug and presses a loud, smacking kiss on the crown of my head. "Hey. Look who's up. Buenos dias, my love."

My father ruffles my hair as he walks by.

"Good morning," I say to both of them, eyeing the Crockpot on the opposite counter, wondering if they're going to notice it before Ava gets up. I picked the Crockpot because of its location. In the mornings, my parents use the appliances on the left, and the Crockpot is on the right, which means they won't catch on to what's about to go down.

"What are you doing up so early?" my father asks, putting his travel mug under the coffeemaker and pressing a button to get the machine going.

I look down at my empty bowl. "I got hungry," I tell him.

"I bet you did. You're just growing and growing, getting taller by the minute." My mother laughs. She goes to open the refrigerator door and stares at its contents.

My father's strong coffee brewing and my mother's bagels popping out of the toaster bring Ava down the stairs. She's dragging her colcha behind her. The thick pink-and-blue quilt our Ita made for her when she was born is special to her and she still sleeps with it. I have one too, only mine is yellow and green, and I don't drag it behind me like a rag because I want it to last forever.

"Can I have some cereal?" Ava asks, rubbing her eyes and pulling the colcha around her shoulders so that it's no longer on the floor.

"Already on it," my father says, pouring milk into a bowl of sugarcoated flakes and dropping a few blueberries over it before setting it on the counter.

As my sister scoots in beside me, I smile at her a little too brightly. I can't help it. I am a bundle of excited nerves, because I am just waiting for the moment she notices what my parents have missed the whole time they've been in the kitchen.

"What's wrong with you?" Ava asks, frowning at me.

I grin. "What are you talking about?"

"You keep looking at me," Ava says.

"Looking at you?" I ask.

My mother pulls the orange juice out of the refrigerator and comes over to pour each of us a glass. "What's going on?" she asks as she puts the juice down in front of us to check the time on her phone.

"He's looking at me," Ava insists.

"We should get going," my father tells my mother. "It takes an hour to get to the university, and we don't know the traffic here."

But my mother is not listening to my father. "He's what?" she asks Ava.

"Looking at me!" Ava repeats.

"What a CROCK!" I say, emphasizing the word and craning my neck to look around the kitchen.

"James"—my father's voice is a warning—"we don't use that . . . word."

"What word? *CROCK?*" I ask. "Why? What's wrong with *CROCK?* It's just a word. CROCK a ham. CROCK some chili. Crock-a-dile. Crock. Crock. Crock."

"James?" My mother puts the bottle of juice back in the refrigerator. "What's wrong with you? Why are you acting like this?"

"Oh, no reason," I say. "Just trying to explain myself."

Ava's eyes narrow. She turns her head left and looks directly at the Crockpot sitting on the counter behind my mother. Then her eyes widen, and her mouth falls wide open.

"James!" she screams as she scrambles off her stool and goes over to save Hermelinda, her small rag doll, who's trapped holding a HELP! sign against the glass lid of our big family-sized Crockpot.

"Oh, James." My mother sighs. "You promised."

"What?" I ask. "I didn't do anything. That doll is possessed! Look at her creepy eyes. I hope she didn't turn the rest of them."

"Stop being mean, James!" Ava holds Hermelinda against her chest and smooths down her long dark hair as she rocks her back and forth, pretending that she still plays with her muñecas. Only I know she's faking it. She's too busy playing Mad Little Scientist in her room to play dolly anymore. "You poor, poor thing. How long have you been trapped in there?"

I snicker.

My father puts his hands on his hips and shakes his head. "Son," he says, and he sounds disappointed. "We talked about this."

"What?" I ask. "It's not like anything got spilled. There's no

34

mess. Just payback. Clean and simple payback."

"You're so mean!" Ava says as she walks out of the kitchen and goes up the stairs with Hermelinda in her arms and her colcha dragging behind her.

My father points a finger at me, and says, "This stops right—"

But he doesn't get to finish his thought, because, upstairs, Ava lets out a bloodcurdling scream that makes my parents put everything down and rush out of the kitchen.

"She's okay," I say, following close behind them.

Ava runs out of her room and stands at the top of the stairs. Her arms are pressed against her body and her hands are balled into fists; she's so angry. "They're gone!" she yells down at our parents. "All of them! Sofia, Nacha, Gloria, Estela . . . all of them. Gone."

"Gone?" I ask them, when our parents turn back to me, their faces frozen in disapproving frowns. "No way. They've got to be here somewhere. You know how malcriadas those dolls are, always getting into mischief."

"Mischief?" My mother's eyes scan the living room, but nothing's afoot there. I made sure of that. Ava's going to have to work hard to find her mischievous muñecas.

"Give them back," my father orders.

"Don't worry," I tell them. "She'll find them soon enough."

I don't tell them about the *scavenger hunt* I have planned for my little sister.

"Where are they!" Ava yells as she runs down the stairs.

I roll my eyes at her. "Stop overreacting. You know I'd never do anything bad to them."

My father huffs and turns around to grab his keys off the hook by the front door. "You two need to figure this out. Your mother and I have to go. We don't have time for this pranking business."

My mother picks her bag off the coffee table and hauls it over her shoulder. "Your father's right. This has to stop." Then she reaches over and hugs and kisses each of us. "You two are getting too old for this. Find the dolls. Call a truce. And be nice to each other."

My father hugs and kisses us too. "Please behave yourselves," he says as he closes the door behind him.

Ava turns to me. "Well?" she says. "Where are they?"

I pull a piece of paper out of my pants pocket and hand it to her. It takes Ava all morning, but thanks to my clever clues and her super-giant, gifted-and-talented scientific brain, she finds every single one of her muñecas.

"I found the last one, no thanks to you," Ava says when she gets back from the koi pond across the street, where Isabel, the last of her missing dolls, was sitting on a bench, feeding bread crumbs to the koi fish.

"Well?" I ask. "Did you have fun?"

Ava frowns as she stands at the bottom of the stairs, hugging Isabel close to her. "No. Why would I?"

"Because some of them were funny," I say, remembering the

muñeca I set up inside Baxter's kennel. She looked like she was eating his dog food.

"Well, nobody wants to find their baby pooping chocolate chips into the bathroom sink. That wasn't funny, James," Ava says. "It was kind of mean, actually."

"What was mean about that?" I ask her.

Ava huffs. "Going bobo? That's kind of personal, don't you think?" she asks.

"Ah, come on. I left her clothes on, and you laughed," I say, clicking through channel after channel and finding nothing to watch on TV.

"I did not!" Ava looks horrified.

I turn off the television and get up. "Don't pretend you didn't," I tell her as I walk around her. "I heard you all the way out here."

"Yeah? Well, maybe I was laughing at the next prank I'm going to play on you," Ava hollers as she follows me upstairs and turns left to go to her room. "Maybe I was planning it all out in my head."

I stand in the hall, watching as my sister props Isabel on the dresser before digging through a box on her bed. "What are you looking for?" I ask.

Ava finds the sign she puts up when she wants to be left alone. She pulls it out and hangs it on her door before she slams it in my face. The words *"KEEP OUT! GENIUS AT WORK!"* do the talking for her.

That's when I realize this is serious. My hands start to sweat,

37

because I know what that sign means—my little sister's on the warpath. She's in there right now, hatching some sneaky little plot to take me down. And I know that whatever it is, it's not going to be pretty, because unlike me, she's not afraid to get her hands dirty.

At lunchtime, I put a sticky note on Ava's door and knock quickly. Then I rush down to the kitchen to make some of my special ham-and-cheese tortas. It's more than a peace offering, it's an honest-to-goodness ofrenda. Because Ava loves my tortas, it's the only chance I have of getting her out of her room so we can try to play nice. My plan works, and soon she is sitting at the counter, eating her favorite meal, but I can see it in her eyes, she's not ready to call a truce.

After lunch, Ava decides it's time to take Baxter for his afternoon walk. Because she knows our parents don't let her go out alone, she lets me tag along. We head down the slope of Pine Circle and turn left again. Baxter barks and jumps and tugs at his leash when he spots the same kids playing ball at the end of Whitebark. "Come on, let's go watch them," Ava says, letting Baxter pull her toward the game.

"Hmm . . . I don't think . . ." I hesitate and look back the way we came, toward Douglas Fir. But Baxter's determined, and Ava is practically running behind him. "Wait up!" I yell as I trot after them.

Ava stops and stands across the street, at the corner of the last house, and watches the game quietly. I walk slowly up to her and take Baxter's leash out of her hand. "Come on," I tell her. "We have to get back."

"Give me a minute," she says. "I'm tired. I need to catch my breath."

"One minute," I tell her firmly, and she nods and crosses her arms in front of her as we stand there, watching the game.

"His posture is all wrong," I tell her. "He needs to widen his stance, bend his knees, and roll up a bit."

"Strike one!" the catcher yells, because there's no umpire.

"His hands need to be closer together," I say as I watch the boy lean in for the second throw. "He needs to use his fingers, not his palms, to grip the bat."

"Strike two!" the catcher yells, after the boy twists himself into a skinny pretzel trying to hit the ball as it crosses the plate.

"He's too far back," I mumble under my breath. "Come on. Don't be afraid."

"Get closer to the plate!" Ava yells, cupping her hands around her mouth, creating a bullhorn effect with them.

"What are you doing?" I ask her as she continues to scream.

"Helping," Ava says, keeping her gaze on the game. "Tuck yourself in—como cochinilla! And put your hands closer together!"

The pitcher throws the ball into his glove and stares at us, which makes the batter turn to give us a sideward glance. He's probably wondering what Ava's talking about and thinking she's just some kind of weird kid.

Only, I know she's not weird. She's explaining how to stand at the plate the same way my father used to explain it to us when he told us to curl up like those little bugs that turn into a tiny ball the minute you touch them.

"Stop," I tell her, tugging on her sleeve, trying to make her quit her hollering. "Ava, please. They don't know what you're saying."

But Ava is too busy coaching the batter to listen to me.

"No! No! Hands lower on the bat! Use your fingertips!" She repeats what I said to her, as the batter's fingers twiddle and drum against the neck of his bat for a moment before he tightens his grip again. "Augh! He's not listening to me."

"Strike three!" the catcher yells, and he stands up and looks over at us before he shakes his head and throws the ball back at the pitcher.

The batter throws the bat aside as he steps away from the plate. He watches us as he starts to walk back to his position as a shortstop. The kids around the diamond shift positions in a way that tells me they've been playing together as a team for a while, using their spare time to hone their skills. They have a routine, fielding their regular positions and taking turns running up to bat.

As the players move, the pitcher hands the ball to his relief, but instead of walking toward home plate to bat, he stands there staring at us. "Hey, can you give it a rest? We know what we're doing. We don't need you harassing us."

"Harassing?" Ava calls back. "How was I harassing you?"

The pitcher starts walking toward us. "You don't scream at the batter," he says when he gets to the edge of the playing field. "It's not nice."

I put my hand on Ava's shoulder, to let her know I'm on her side.

"Don't get mad at her," I tell the pitcher across the street. "She's just trying to help."

"Help?" the pitcher asks. "She's not making any sense. '*Tuck yourself in*'? What does that even mean? So dumb."

"He was standing too straight," Ava says defensively.

"His back was too stiff," I explain. "He needs to roll up a bit."

The kids in the field start walking over to the edge of the street. They hang back a bit, behind the pitcher, who is clearly their leader.

"Como cochinilla!" Ava yells again, pointing at me with her thumb. "Listen to him. He's the best hitter on our team in Texas."

"Shh," I tell Ava. "Stop. You're embarrassing me."

The pitcher narrows his eyes as he stares at me. "A what?"

"A pill bug," I tell him. "You gotta bend at the knees, but also curl up a bit like a roly-poly. It helps the swing."

The kids behind the pitcher cup their hands over their mouths, mumble things to one another, and laugh.

"Come on, roly-poly, come show us!"

"Yeah, bug boy, show us what you got!"

"Curl up, bug boy!"

41

"Roly-poly!"

As the boys yell, the pitcher stares at me.

"Well?" he finally asks when I stare back at him without answering his team's tauntings. "You gonna get up to bat, or what?"

"Go!" Ava puts her hand on my back and pushes me forward gently. "Show them how it's done, James."

The pitcher stares at me, unblinking, challenging me, daring me to prove I know what I'm talking about. But I do know what I'm talking about, and I refuse to back down because backing down would be like disrespecting the life I had in Texas, like erasing everything Beto and Mike and I ever accomplished together.

Sensing an opportunity to move, Baxter barks and jumps around in front of me. I break the stare war between me and the pitcher long enough to hand Ava his leash.

"Wait here," I say as I trot across the street.

As I saunter over to home plate, I can hear Baxter's excited snorting as he and Ava follow me across the street, but I don't turn around to look at them. My eyes are focused on the bat lying on the ground. It's nothing special, just a department store bat, but I could make a twisted twig work when it comes to hitting the ball. This is my specialty. This is what I'm good at.

I wrap my fingers around the base of the bat, stand with my feet more than shoulder-width apart, bend my knees, and curl up a bit, just like my father taught me.

The pitcher takes the mound and stares at me.

I practice hitting the ball, stretching out my arms every time. My heart is racing, roaring against my eardrums, and my hands are sweating. I haven't held a bat in weeks, not since I told Coach I wouldn't be coming back next year.

The pitcher fixes his cap, pulls it off, puts it back on.

I catch a glimpse of blond hair, stare at his glove, calculate distance, predict depth, and wipe my hands on my pants before I position myself for that first pitch.

He pulls his arm back, lifts his leg, and sends a fast one toward me.

I pull back and swing with all my might.

Plop! The ball goes flying in the air, a white blur making its way to the dark tree line with silent speed.

"Whoa!"

"Yeah!"

"Dang!"

"What was that?"

Their remarks reach my ears, but I am not looking back. I'm running around the bases as fast as I can, not because I don't know it's a home run but because I want them to see I can run too. I want them to know everything I can do in this game— before they find out I don't always catch a fly ball and I won't steal any bases.

"Yes! Yes!" Ava screams as she and Baxter jump up and down and cheer for me from the sidelines. "I told you! You have to curl up—como cochinilla!"

But Ava and Baxter aren't the only ones cheering for me. All the kids on that field run up to congratulate me. They slap my shoulders with their gloves and fist bump one another.

"That was killer!"

"You've got to join our team!"

"We'll crush the Bears if you join us!"

"We'll win the World Series!"

"I'll just be happy if we win one game for a change," the catcher says.

I accept their happy slaps on the back, their smiles, their surprise at my skills with the bat.

"Hey, that was great," the pitcher says. "I'm Jack. What's your name?"

"James," Ava says, while Baxter leaps in circles, wrapping his leash around my legs. "And I'm Ava. James and Ava McNichols. We live on Pine Circle."

"The new kids," the catcher says. "I'm Ronnie. This is Paul, Laurie, Sam, and Beth. Those two are Daniel and Dave. They're twins, and that's their cousin Stephanie. She can hit too. I mean, she's not a big hitter like you. But she gets herself on base every time."

"Too bad nobody ever gets her home," Daniel whispers under his breath.

"Guys, guys," Ronnie says. "Let's keep this positive, okay?"

"So, I guess you don't win many games," Ava says, and everyone turns to look at her.

Then, because nobody says anything, Jack shrugs his shoulders and says, "We're not awful . . . but it would be nice if you joined our team. We could use a good hitter."

"Oh, James is more than that," Ava says. "He's fantastic. Every ball he hits goes over the fence. And he hits all of them. Every time. For sure."

Embarrassed, I cut Ava off.

"I'm glad to meet you," I say, turning around several times to untangle myself from Baxter's leash. "Sorry, he gets really excited."

"What's your dog's name?" Jack asks.

"Baxter." Ava takes the leash back from me. "And he's my dog, not James's."

"Well?" Stephanie asks. "Are you two going to join our team?"

"Oh, no, not me," Ava says. "I'm more of a nature person, a scientist. And there's lots of specimens to examine out here before I decide on this year's science project. I don't have time for games."

"That's fair," Stephanie says. "How about you?"

"You have to join," Daniel says. "We need someone to help us bring Stephanie home. She always gets stuck between second and third."

Their requests make me think of Beto and Mike, playing without me back home, and my chest starts to hurt again, a dull ache that I can't ignore.

"I don't know," I say. "I haven't decided if I want to get involved in Little League this year. We just got here. So, I'm taking it slow.

Not making any big decisions yet."

"How about oatmeal cookies?" Jack asks. "Can you commit to that?"

"What?" I ask, confused.

"Our moms bake cookies for us to share after every practice," Beth says. "They take turns."

"My mom makes oatmeal cookies on Wednesdays," Jack says. "We're heading that way right now. Wanna come over?"

"I'm always up for cookies," Ava says, eyes sparkling as she looks up at me. "What do you think? Can we go?"

CHAPTER 4

I've never really liked oatmeal cookies, but on Wednesday afternoon Jack's mom made a believer out of me. Now I love oatmeal cookies! However, Beth's mom, Mrs. Martin, makes the best sugar cookies. She takes her time and decorates them like little baseballs, gloves, and home plates. They're pretty cool, and the icing is flavored, so they're extra good.

Walking back home from Beth's house on Thursday, Ava holds a huge baseball cookie carefully in her hands.

"Are you gonna eat that?" I ask her.

"Nope. It's not for eating," she says. "I'm going to make an ornament out of it."

"You're going to hang food on our tree?" I ask her because Christmas is, like, five months away. "Well, let's hope it doesn't crumble and fall apart before that."

Ava giggles. "I'm going to preserve it, silly."

"Well, sugar ants won't care if it's preserved," I tell her.

"Seriously, how are you going to keep it from the ants?"

"I'm a scientist," Ava proclaims. "I'll find a way."

I think about the huge hydroponics science project Ava put together with my father last year, and I know she's not lying. I've never seen so many plants grow so big without soil before. If there's a way of keeping that cookie intact for the rest of her life, Ava will find it.

"I'm sure you will," I tell her. "But let me know if you change your mind. I'll eat it if you don't want it."

"I'm sure you'll have plenty of cookies to eat," Ava says. "You are joining the team, right?"

I think of Beto and Mike, and I wonder how they feel about playing without me this year. I haven't asked them, because, well, that's not the kind of thing we talk about. Mostly, we just pick on each other. Beto can throw a ball all the way back from left field, but he can't run very fast, and Mike's a great runner, but he hasn't hit more than a few home runs in his life.

"Well?" Ava asks.

"I'm not sure," I say. "I haven't decided."

Ava stops and turns to face me at the corner. "Come on, James, you have to join. Jack and them are depending on you. They're our friends now. Plus, there are serious perks to being on the team."

"Oh, yeah?" I ask, because I know all about the team. Jack filled me in while Ava chatted up some of the other kids before the game today.

Ava rolls her eyes.

"Yes," she says. "Beth and Laurie told me they have all kinds of cool fund-raisers to get the money for uniforms, and Stephanie says they even have a float in the Spring Parade. This place is great, James! How can you not want to be part of it?"

Ava's enthusiasm makes me smile. Oregon's really growing on her. I look at the giant baseball cookie in her hand. Treats after every practice, a carnival booth, a car wash, and a float in the Spring Parade all sound like a lot of fun.

"It is a really cool place to be, isn't it?" I ask her, and she grins and nods.

"Okay," I say. "I'll think about it."

When we get home, I go to my room to change out of my clothes. I take off my shoes and put them in their cubby in the closet and turn back to unpack my gym bag on the bed. Suddenly, a strong, angry wind comes in through the window.

Funny, but I don't remember leaving it open.

I sprint across the room to close the window, but the frame is stuck, and I have to pull on it hard before I can bring it all the way down. When I'm done smoothing down the curtains, I turn to my desk and reach for one of my baseball magazines. But then I notice a square, ancient-looking envelope propped up on my keyboard, against my computer screen.

Weird. I don't remember seeing it there before.

How could I have missed it? It's sitting in plain sight, right in front of me. But how did it get there? For some reason, the sight

49

of the strange envelope makes the tiny hairs on my forearms rise up, and I rub at the goose bumps vigorously. I don't know why, but I get a strange feeling that I am not alone. I peek over my shoulder and glance around the room, looking for whatever is giving me the chills.

But there is no one there.

Because *I am alone* in my room.

So, I reach over, pick it up, and hold the weighty envelope in my hand. This is no ordinary paper. It looks old-fashioned, like those documents you see under a glass case in the museum. I test its texture against my fingertips and stare at the writing on the front of the envelope.

~~James Anthony McNichols~~

My name, big and bold in black ink, is written in some kind of old-style script, like something out of the Middle Ages. And when I turn it over, I see that the fancy envelope is secured by a real, honest-to-goodness wax seal, pressed firmly onto the back.

An invitation? I wonder as I trace the strange seal gently with my fingertips and outline the emblem—four tiny triangular symbols in a circle around a larger fifth symbol in the center. Gingerly, I tug at the seal. It's really stuck on, so I tug a bit harder. A small part of it gives way, and I tug again, harder this time, tearing it off the envelope in one fell swoop. I open it. The message inside is written in the same long, elegant letters.

Dear James,

I am glad you are settling in to your new home. It's nice to see a youngblood living in it again. I saw you wandering from room to room.

As the last in a long line of Guardians of your house, let me assure you, the house is perfect— as magnificently conceived as every house on Pine Circle. The question is, do you belong here? Are you worthy of it?

Like this community, your house is very special. Go ahead, explore it, try to uncover its many secrets. Just don't break anything. I'm watching you.

The Keeper

I blink and stare at the letter that trembles in my unsteady hand.

Youngblood! Long line of Guardians! The Keeper!

Every word, every phrase, every sentence spelled out in that strange letter sends a chill down my spine, and for a moment I can't breathe. I close my eyes, and when I open them I read the letter again. Only this time, other words jump out at me, spitting their poison at my eyes like cobras.

Do you belong? Are you worthy? I'm watching you!

Watching!

Me?

Why?

My mind races even as my head spins, and I can feel my heartbeat racing, thrumming in my temples. *What does this mean? Who would send me this?* I keep asking myself.

"Mom, Dad," I mumble as I stand there, unable to move my legs much less scream out for my parents to come upstairs so I can show them the creepy letter.

Don't panic, I tell myself. *This isn't real. Maybe one of the neighborhood kids, someone not on Jack's team, is playing tricks. It's some kind of practical joke. It has to be. But what kind of person would do this to a kid they don't even know yet?*

I turn the letter over and over in my hands. There is no return address. No stamp. No markings from the post office. Just my full name. Centered on the parchment. In that fancy, ancient-looking handwriting.

Ava! my mind screams.

Of course.

This would be funny, even cool, if I was in a mood to keep our prank war going. *But how did she do this so quickly?* I ask myself. *She must have been planning this one for weeks, looking up big words in her huge thesaurus.* That wouldn't surprise me. She's more than smart—my sister is a little imp! *But I'm not playing by her rules. I decide when and where this prank war goes,* I tell myself, and I toss the letter in the trash can I keep by my desk and walk away.

That afternoon, when I tell our parents about Jack and his team, they are so excited about the possibility of having me join Little League again that they start making all kinds of plans. After dinner, my father makes a call and gets in touch with Beth's father, Mr. Martin, because he's coaching their team.

"Just to inquire. No harm in that," he says when I groan about it. And even though it makes me a little uncomfortable, Friday afternoon my parents decide to walk Baxter down to the baseball field with us to watch me play a game with Jack's team. Ava goes on and on, excitedly, and my parents hang on her every word.

"They asked me to play too," she says. "But I told them I'm more of a science-and-numbers person. I said I'd just watch and document what I think each person needs to work on. That way, I can come up with a strategy for them to get better."

"A strategy?" my mother asks. "What kind of strategy?"

"You know," Ava says. "Like a plan for the team—who needs to work on what. I've already noticed that Daniel is fast. He moves quickly toward the ball, but his brother, Dave, is a little slow. So, Dave needs to work on that. And Stephanie can hit the ball two out of three times, which is good, but she needs to work on putting some power behind it. James can help her with that. He'll show her what to do."

53

"Hmm . . . ," my father says. "Sounds like you're onto something there, Coach."

"I am," Ava says. "I'll have the team in shape way before the season starts."

"So, you like playing with this team?" My father turns to look at me, and I take a deep breath.

"I'm not sure. I don't know them that well, yet," I say, shaking my head and looking at the ground in front of me, because I am still pretty confused about how I feel playing out here—without Beto and Mike. *I mean, what am I going to tell them? That I'm joining another team? That I'm showing others our special moves? That I'm giving away our secrets to winning? I don't want them to think I'm a traitor!*

My parents stop at the edge of the street and wave at the kids who are already there, tossing the ball around, warming up. I drop my gym bag on the ground, unzip it, pull out my favorite bat, and grab my glove.

Ava watches me intensely as I stand up.

"What? Something wrong with my technique?" I ask, teasing her as I straighten my ball cap and push it farther down on the back of my head.

Ava opens the small notebook she's taken out of her backpack and shakes her head. "Nope," she says. Then she grins and props her pencil over the page, to show that she's ready to start taking notes.

"Have a good game," my father says as I put my bat under

my arm and start to put my hand into my glove, because I'm taking the field first.

"We won't stay long. We still have to walk Baxter," my mother promises, but I am not listening to her, because something's not right with my glove.

At first, I think it's my imagination, but the inside of my glove feels wet, and my fingers are already deep inside it before I realize it.

"Ava!" I scream when I pull my fingers out of the glove and see that they are covered in something gooey and slimy and completely transparent.

My mother takes a short, horrified breath.

"Here, hold your chucho," my mother tells Ava as she hands Baxter's leash to her. Then she takes the glove out of my hand to inspect it. "Let me see that."

"What in the world?" My father touches the gooey gunk slathered all over my hand. He feels the texture of it on his fingertips and sniffs it.

"Petroleum jelly!" my mother whispers, looking down at Ava, who is practically jumping up and down on her tiptoes with excitement.

"Ha!" she says, and she punctuates the word SCORE on her notebook with an exclamation point and shows it to me. "Got you back! You should have seen your face, James. You were not expecting that at all!"

"Ava, this isn't funny," my mother says, opening up the glove wider and trying to see how much petroleum jelly is inside it.

"But it was!" Ava says. "And he deserved it, for kidnapping my dolls!"

"But that wasn't mean—" I whine as my mother looks through Ava's backpack and finds the small package of wet wipes she put there for my little sister. She used to do the same thing for me, but I made her stop when I started middle school and switched from a backpack to a gym bag.

While my mother wipes my hand, my father takes some of the wipes and starts to dig the petroleum jelly out of my glove. "It's no use," he says. "I can't get all this out right now."

I take a few more wet wipes from my mother and clean the rest of the petroleum jelly off my hand. But no matter how hard I scrub, I can still feel the slippery film on my fingers.

"James?" Jack calls out to me. "You okay?"

I turn around and see him walking toward us.

"Don't say anything," I tell Ava. Then, turning back to Jack, I yell, "Yeah. I'm fine. Wait there. I'll be right over."

"But what about your glove?" my mother asks. "You can't play without a glove."

"Maybe one of the boys will lend you one," my father says, and I nod.

Ava points at the bag on the ground between us.

"It's okay," she whispers. "I put your old glove in there. In the side pocket."

I look at her hopeful, wide eyes and see that she's trying to make amends, but my fingers still feel slippery, so I'm not ready to forgive her just yet. "Well, I hope I can get a good grip on the bat," I tell her as I dig my old glove out of my bag.

Turning away from my family, I look back at Jack. He's standing on the other side of the street, watching me. He looks worried, and my stomach twists inside me, because this is the last thing I wanted. Telling Beto and Mike about my sister's latest prank is one thing. They get it that we like to prank each other, that it's all a big game we play, a game that sometimes goes too far, but Jack doesn't know that. And he might get the wrong idea about all this. I don't want him or any of these kids judging Ava. She's my sister, and I love her. I don't want anyone disliking her.

I run across the street and join Jack.

"Hey, you ready?" he asks, and I nod.

From right field, I see Stephanie hit the ball. It's heading my way. But I don't panic, because it's a grounder, so I know I can get it. I run toward it, catch it, and throw it to first base, but Stephanie makes it there first and she's safe.

Daniel bats next, and though he doesn't hit the ball, Stephanie takes the opportunity to steal second base. I watch her sprint off, like a cheetah, moving so quickly that she's on the ground and touching the base before I can adjust my cap. And I have to admit I'm kind of jealous. I just can't steal a base. It's too risky.

On the sideline, Ava jots something down in her notepad. Across the street, my parents clap while Baxter sniffs the air and looks at a bird overhead. I'm up next, so I trot over to home plate, drop my glove, and grab the bat. My fingers as I grip the bat are slimy and icky and gross. I can feel the petroleum jelly clogging every pore of my skin, and I worry that my hands will slip when I swing the bat around.

On the mound, Jack throws the ball into his glove again and again. He twists his neck. I practice my swing and feel the slippery residue of petroleum jelly messing with my grip. I take a step back and scrub my hands hard against my jeans. But it's no use—I can't get the slimy stuff off my hands. I don't want to hold up the game any longer, so I nod for Jack to throw the ball.

Jack lifts his leg and throws a fastball. I see it coming like I see all balls coming, in slow motion, perfectly aligned with my body, coming straight into my comfort zone, and I raise my bat and swing.

"Strike!" Ronnie calls it, and I drop the bat, startled. My vision blurs, and my blood races through my veins so fast, I feel a bit dizzy. I close my eyes, take a deep breath, and let it out slowly through my mouth.

Did I really just miss that? I haven't missed a ball for two whole seasons! It's like some kind of record in Little League back home. Stupid petroleum jelly. Stupid prank. Ava has no idea what she's done. She has no idea what this means for me.

I open my eyes again and look over at my sister on the sideline. She's not writing anything down on her notebook anymore. In fact, she's standing there, biting her lip and staring at me like

I've just grown hooves and a tail. The sight of her, acting all worried, makes me mad, and I turn my eyes away from her.

"You okay?" Ronnie asks.

I blink. Swallow. Nod. Before Jack or any of the others can say anything, I pick up my bat again. Holding it up, I take a few more breaths, in, out, in, out, until I can feel my heartbeat slowing down.

I can do this, I tell myself as I bend my knees and roll my body into it, like a cochinilla. *There is no petroleum jelly on my fingers. There is no petroleum jelly on my bat. There is no petroleum jelly strong enough to stop me from hitting a home run again!*

"Strike two!" Ronnie yells.

I lower my bat and look over at my parents. They are smiling, tight little smiles that say, *We are not really worried.* Only I know better. There is no other way to read those tiny tense grins.

Ronnie stands up and stares at Jack. "You're getting better," he says. Then, because he sees that I am mortified, he raises his eyebrows at me and says, "Don't worry, you'll get the next one."

I grip the bat with my fingers, roll my palms over it, and then, just to be sure, I bring it up to my nose and sniff it. It's no use. I can smell the petroleum on it. It's there, slippery and slimy and icky. I take a deep breath, but all I want to do at this moment—when I realize I might not hit the next ball, when I realize I might strike out altogether—is take my bat to the sideline and rub dirt all over it. So, I do it. I step back and scrub my bat with soil and sand and grit until I can grip it with confidence.

"Strike three!" Ronnie yells. "You're out!"

"What?" I ask, because I never saw the ball coming. It happened so fast, too fast, and I missed it altogether. "I wasn't ready," I tell Ronnie. "I wasn't ready," I tell Jack.

"It's okay," Ronnie says. "You'll hit it next time."

But I never strike out! I want to scream. *I never miss. I don't always catch the fly balls, and I won't steal a base, but I always hit the ball over the fence. It's my only gift. It's my only talent. Ava has science and math and formulas and numbers, but I have this. I have baseball.*

I look back at my parents. They're clapping. *Clapping! Really? Why are they clapping?* Tears start to prick at the back of my eyes, because I'm beyond embarrassed. I feel hurt, and worried, and ashamed, because the tears are threatening to burst out of my eyes and roll down my face. But I can't let that happen, so I force them back. Then I step away from the plate and toss my bat off to the side, with the rest of the bats.

"It's okay," Jack says as he hands me my old glove, and I step aside because he's next up to bat. "You don't expect to hit every ball, do you? That's just crazy. Don't put that kinda pressure on yourself. It's not good."

I turn away from Jack and Ronnie. *They don't understand. Nobody understands. This is the end of my streak. This is the end of my record. What am I going to tell Beto and Mike when they bring up how their season is going? That I struck out? That I'm a loser out here? Will they get it? How bad this is for me? How bad*

I feel? Will they tease me about it? Tell me I had to come all the way across the country to strike out? Or will they just be happy because I'm not helping another team win?

When we get home, my parents are quiet. Except for a couple of pats on the back and a few "Good job" comments, they decide not to make a big deal of it, and they go into the kitchen to start cooking dinner. Even Ava knows better than to say anything while she butters the French bread slices and hands them to me so I can sprinkle them with garlic before we put them in the oven.

Ava didn't just mess up my game, she crossed the line and she knows it. Just because her stupid letter didn't scare me doesn't mean she gets another try. She should have left well enough alone, and I've given her enough mean stares to let her know it's better if she lets me get over this by myself.

After dinner, Stephanie and her mother, Mrs. Johnson, come knocking on our door with our next-door neighbor Mrs. Martin. When I open the door, Stephanie is standing there, holding a plateful of brownies. Mrs. Johnson is behind her, holding a gift basket.

"This is your share of today's treats," Stephanie says as she hands them to me.

"I hope you don't mind us dropping by," Mrs. Johnson says. "Stephanie wanted to make sure you didn't miss out on my specialty."

Surprised, I take the plastic-wrapped plate and step aside to let them all in. "No, I don't mind," I tell her.

"Come in," Ava says as she stands in the hallway. "Ooooooh, brownies!"

My mother comes out of the kitchen and takes the giant gift basket Mrs. Martin is holding in her hands. "Oh, my goodness. You didn't have to do this," my mother says, turning the basket around to admire it.

"It's nothing," Mrs. Martin says. "Just a few apricot scones, fresh berries, and my specialty, orange-blossom tea."

"Wow! It looks amazing." My mother grins.

"And expensive," Ava says.

"Oh, no." Mrs. Martin waves a hand in the air and shakes her head. "Everything you see there comes from our community garden, down by the pond. Oh, except for the tea, that's from my own personal herb garden. It's very nice before bed. I used to give it to my children when they couldn't sleep."

"Well, that was very thoughtful of you," my father says, standing up from his throne in the living room. Then, looking at my mother, he says, "I'm going to work in the office a bit. You ladies have a nice evening."

My mother walks with Mrs. Martin and Mrs. Johnson into the kitchen.

I put the plateful of brownies on the coffee table and plop myself on the couch and turn the volume down on the television set, so that they can talk without having to yell at each other.

Stephanie and Ava sit on the love seat. My sister unwraps the plate of brownies and offers it to me. I take a brownie and bite into it. Of course, it's good—more than good, it's great, with tiny marshmallows and bits of pecans and caramel. It's the best brownie I've ever had. I take a second bite as I click on the remote control, scrolling through the menu, trying to find something good for us to watch after dinner.

"The whole neighborhood is excited about tomorrow's barbecue," I hear Mrs. Johnson tell my mother. "I'm making my famous lemon meringue pie."

"The barbecue!" Ava squeals. "Oh, I forgot about that!"

Stephanie nods. "It's tomorrow afternoon."

How could she forget? I ask myself. *It's in the grassy area out here, in front of our house, where I posed several of her dolls on the picnic tables and koi pond.* I smile to myself as I remember my prank. I spent a lot of time and energy on it, but it was so much fun putting her dolls in all kinds of mischievous poses. So, it was worth it.

Now, why couldn't Ava do that? Why couldn't she stick to the rules—one prank at a time, make it fun but harmless? Why couldn't she be a good prankster without being mean? Remembering the way my parents looked at me when I struck out makes me so mad. Rage starts to build up inside me, and I can feel my eyes prick with tears again. But I force it all down. It's no use blowing up about it now. It won't change anything.

It doesn't matter, I tell myself as I push the memory of my first strikeout in two years away, because I've made up my mind. *My next prank is going to be epic. Ava's going to be sorry she ruined my glove and my game!*

CHAPTER 5

Instead of watching TV with the family after dinner, I spend all evening lying on the roof outside my window, watching Ita's videos where she's giving us consejos.

"Take care of each other," my Ita says. Because she dresses up for our videos, she is wearing a blue dress with red embroidered flowers on the neckline and shoulders, and her white hair is braided and pinned neatly on top of her head. Her dark eyes sparkle and crinkle at the corners, and she smiles at me as I hold the camera in front of her. *"Whatever happens, always remember you are brother and sister, and there's nothing more precious, nothing more important, than family. Now go home. Go play with your sister. Hug her. Smooch her. Challenge and spook her—keep her on her toes for me, will ya!"*

The video wobbles as I move off her hospital bed right before I press down on the record button. Surprised, I hit play and watch the video again, and it's right there, at the end, right before I jump off the bed.

"Keep her on her toes for me, will ya!"

It's funny, but I don't remember her saying that to me. Though it makes sense, because our Ita used to play all kinds of little tricks on us. When we played hide-and-seek, she'd jump out of closets or from behind curtained windows and yell, *"Cucuy!"* And when we screamed, she'd grab us and say, *"It's just me, keeping you on your toes!"* Then she'd hug us and squeeze us and kiss us until the susto, the scare that stole our breaths and made us tremble, was all gone because she loved it all away.

She was the best abuelita ever!

"Keep her on her toes for me," she says when I press play again, and I laugh, because I can't help but feel like this prank war Ava and I have going on is all her fault. She taught us that it's okay to play fun tricks on each other as long as nobody gets hurt.

"Oh, don't worry, I will," I say as I turn off the screen, lay the phone on my chest, and stare at the stars. Though I'm not mad at Ava anymore, I still have this need to get back at her, to give my little sister a good old susto and let her know who the Ultimate Prankmaster really is, once and for all.

Beto sends me a text message, and I go back into my room to chat with him and Mike. I consider not telling them about Ava's latest prank because I don't know what they'll say when I tell them I'm joining a team up here. But, to my surprise, they are both okay with it.

BETO: that's so cool
that you found a team
to play with up there
ME: really?
BETO: yeah . . . you gotta keep your
swing muscle strong
MIKE: gotta stay in the game
can't let your skills go
not skills like yours anyway
ME: what about you? you guys getting
ready down there?
MIKE: definitely
BETO: oh yeah.
practicing with the guys every day
just like always

With a sense of relief, I lie in bed wondering what I can do to get Ava back for ruining my record. Frustrated, because I honestly can't think of anything special enough, I take out my phone and start looking online for inspiration.

"This is really sad," I tell Baxter when he comes into my room, jumps on the bed, and curls up next to me. "Why did Ava have to get all the creative genes in this family, huh? It's not fair, is it, boy?"

Baxter sniffs at the phone in my hand, whines, and nuzzles my neck.

"What did you say, boy?" I ask him, cringing when he licks my earlobe. "You want to help? Why, thank you! I knew you loved me best. Let's see if we can find something we can do together—really pay Ava back for ruining my game!"

It takes me a while, but I finally hit on the best prank idea I've ever seen. It's so good because it fits Ava perfectly, but also because I can't stop laughing every time I watch it. Baxter looks a little bored when I show it to him, but I know exactly what to do to make him the star of my prank!

When everyone goes to bed, I spend hours working in the dark with nothing but my flashlight to light my creation because I don't want anyone in the house to see what I'm doing. By the time I'm done, I am exhausted. But it doesn't matter, because this is my masterpiece—the prank to outdo all other pranks. Ava won't see this one coming.

I don't go to sleep until after three a.m., and when I wake up to the scent of something warm and spicy and delicious wafting up the stairs, I sit up in bed, scratch my head, and look around the room. The door is closed and, except for the used-up roll of black electrical tape and scissors sitting on my desk, nothing else is out of order in my room. There is no evidence anywhere of what I was up to in here last night. I did it. I created a masterpiece! Now I have to make sure nobody goes into my closet for the next twenty-four hours.

This is not hard, because it's actually a lot later than I thought. Yes, it's Saturday, and yes, we all sleep late on Saturdays, but by the time I get downstairs it's almost eleven, and my plate of waffles is sitting under a glass dome on the counter.

"Well," Ava says when she sees me come through the living room. "It's about time you got up."

"Where is everybody?" I ask, taking a stool at the counter and pulling my plate toward me. My waffles are cold, but they are still good.

"Dad went into town to get some lawn chairs and one of those big umbrellas so we can sit out there in the quad, and Mom's outside, helping the neighbors set up for the barbecue." Ava keeps her eyes on the television. She pets Baxter's head and ignores me as I scarf my food down.

"The barbecue," I say. "What time does it start?"

"I dunno," Ava says. "I'm supposed to stay in here, to make sure the pie doesn't burn."

"Pie?" I ask.

"Apple. Homemade," Ava says. "Mom just popped it in the oven. So, it'll be a while."

Baxter stands up. He shakes his whole body, yawns, jumps off the couch, and comes over to see if I'll give him a forkful of waffles. I turn to make sure Ava isn't watching me before I slip him a tiny piece of bacon off my plate.

"I saw that," Ava says, her voice annoyed.

"Saw what?" I ask her.

Ava twists around on the couch and stares at me. "He doesn't love you," she says. "He just wants your food."

"He does so love me," I tell her. "He'd do anything for me. Wouldn't you, boy? Wouldn't you do anything for me?"

Baxter goes crazy. He jumps up, puts his paws on my chest, and tries to lick my face off. I pet him and struggle against him, because he's just loving all this attention.

"Stop it, James!" Ava demands. "Stop teasing him with your bacon breath!"

"What?" I ask Baxter. "You wanna go upstairs? You wanna play without Ava? Oh, okay. Let's go. Let's go play in my room."

I put my plate in the soapy water in the sink where the morning dishes are soaking and run across the living room past Ava with Baxter jumping all around me.

"Baxter!" Ava calls. "Come here, boy. Come sit down here with me."

"No, Baxter," I say. "Come here with me. Come on. Let's go upstairs."

We keep it up, calling for Baxter's attention, back and forth, again and again. Baxter looks from one to the other and then, as if having made his decision, he runs out into the hall and stands by the stairs, wagging his tail.

"Ha!" I tell Ava. "He loves me more!"

And I run out of the living room and bound up the stairs before Ava can jump off the couch to follow us. The pie duties keep Ava down in the living room, and I close my bedroom door behind me and Baxter, who jumps on the bed and makes himself into a donut beside me.

"I love you so much!" I tell Baxter as I pull him up to snuggle with me. "I do. You're my favorite chucho in the whole wide world."

While I lie there, I text Beto and Mike, but neither of them answers me, so I go through my photo gallery and laugh at the pictures I took of Ava's mischievous muñecas. That never gets old. "That was a good one." I show Baxter the doll by the koi pond. "But not as good as the one I have planned for tomorrow. And you're going to help me pull it off, aren't you, boy? Yes, you are. You are."

Baxter wiggles his eyebrows up and down as if he's trying to figure out what I'm talking about. The thought of having Ava's dog play a big part in the most excellent prank of all time fills me with excitement, and I sit up in bed.

"Hey, you wanna see if it fits?" I whisper to Baxter, and then, because he doesn't complain, I jump off the bed and head for the closet. "Now, remember, it's not ready, okay? I haven't put the finishing touches on it. I'm gonna do that after everyone goes to sleep tonight. But it's good to try it on. We have to make sure it fits, right?"

I put Baxter into the homemade costume. It fits perfectly. The black-and-red-striped socks I attached to his black harness hug his long, skinny legs. And the extra four shiny legs I created out of paper wrapped with black electrical tape look long and spindly. They wobble and bounce up and down when Baxter walks around the room, dragging my old bean bag behind him like a giant spider's abdomen.

"Wait here," I tell Baxter, when I see that I missed a spot when I was covering up the weak seams on the bean bag with electric tape. "I have to get a new roll. Sit, boy. Stay."

Baxter starts to sit back, but the abdomen is in his way, so he tries to shake it off. When that doesn't work, he starts trying to bite it, but no matter which way he turns the bag goes with him, and so he just gives up and stands there staring at me.

"Good dog!" I tell him. "I'll be right back."

Giggling, I rush across the hall and go into my parents' room. Because I taped his tags against his collar, I don't hear Baxter leaving my bedroom. He's almost to the stairs, his giant abdomen dragging behind him, before I spot him.

Panicked, I rush out of my parents' room and try to cut him off, but I am too late. Baxter is already heading downstairs. The four shiny fake legs wobble up and down and the light abdomen bumps quietly against each step as he "walks" down the circular staircase slowly, like he doesn't know how to move in his spider costume.

"Baxter!" I hiss, from the top of the stairs. "Baxter, get back here!"

Only Baxter isn't listening.

I step onto the third stair and crouch. I put my hands on the railing and peer out into the living room, so that Ava can't see me when Baxter turns the corner and walks up to her on the couch. This is not the way I planned this prank to go down, but if it has to happen like this, then I guess I'm going to have to work with it. I stay put and watch, because I can't give it away, not yet. Not until I give Ava a good scare, to "keep her on her toes"!

Unaware, Ava pauses the show on TV and turns around to look at Baxter. Only it's not Baxter at all. It's Spiderdog coming toward her. She sits up and lets out a bloodcurdling scream.

Spiderdog stops and stares at her.

Still screaming, Ava falls off the couch, scrambles off the floor, and runs out the front door before I can say, *"Wait!"*

I run down the rest of the stairs, but before I can stop him, Baxter gets out of the house without his leash. He rushes out the front door behind Ava. The whole thing happens so fast, I have no time to do anything else but run after them.

I try to catch up to her, but Ava's ponytails are flying behind her as she runs toward my mother, screaming, "Help! Help!" with Spiderdog trotting behind her, his long, shiny Spiderdog legs flopping up and down all around him, giving him the appearance of being an honest-to-goodness giant arachnid.

"Ahhhh!"

"My God!!"

"What is that?!"

"Run!"

"Run!!"

The kids on the grassy knoll in front of our house scream and spread out in all directions, getting out of Spiderdog's way. Parents grab their children. Some of the older kids run off toward their houses. Others jump on the picnic tables. Jack and Ronnie pick up bats and walk backward, holding their bats up defensively, as Spiderdog walks around the grounds, sniffing the air for the scent of meat barbecuing on the grill and looking around, confused by the screaming people scrambling to get away from him.

"Stop!" I tell Jack as I put myself between him and Spiderdog. "It's a prank. It's our chucho, Baxter. Don't hurt him, please!"

My mother, holding a trembling Ava in her arms, glares at me from a few yards away. "Baxter!" she screams, in disbelief.

Thinking he's in trouble, Baxter runs away from us. He bounces off and crawls under the bench of a picnic table and tries to hide. But he gets stuck there, because the bulging beanbag buckled around his abdomen can't go through as easily as the rest of his skinny body, no matter how hard he tugs and pulls.

"Baxter?"

Still clinging to my mother's waist, Ava turns around and watches Spiderdog waggle and wiggle against the iron braces holding up the picnic bench. Desperate to get through to the other side, Spiderdog stretches and strains and, before we know it, he is free. As free as the hundreds of thousands of fluffy gray pellets that burst out of the bag, spill, roll, and get picked up by the wind, taking flight, like tiny spiderling eggs, making kids jump off the tables and run away screaming again.

The pellets go everywhere. They roll over grass and cement. They creep onto picnic tables, crawl under benches, cling to toys, and get caught in kids' hair and clothes, causing pande-monium everywhere they land as people swat and swipe and scream, trying to get them off themselves.

Even Jack's father, Mr. Harvey, can't keep them off the chicken because he closes the grill too late.

"Guys! Guys!" I yell after them. "It's okay. It's just my dog!"

"No!" Ava screams at me as she leaves my mother's side to run toward Baxter. "He's my dog. Baxter is mine. And you did this to him, James! You traumatized him!"

"Oh, poor baby," I hear Beth say as she jumps off a picnic table and starts walking around it with Ava, trying to get Baxter to come out of hiding.

"Come here, baby."

"Come here, boy."

I look around at the chaos I've caused, and the blood rushes up to my face. I can feel my cheeks flush, not because I'm embar-rassed but because I feel ashamed of myself. *How could I do this? How could I let things go so far?*

CHAPTER 6

Even though things have calmed down and everyone's being real nice, I still feel awkward as I help Mrs. Benson clear away the big mess under the picnic table. The neighborhood kids walk around with their parents holding plastic grocery bags and picking up as many of the little gray pellets of stuffing that made their way into every nook and cranny of the grassy knoll and into the barbecue pit.

Ava and Stephanie walk with Mrs. Johnson to her house to get more chicken because this batch is ruined. Mrs. Benson is super nice about the whole thing. Instead of making a fuss, she pats my shoulder and tells me to let it go. Then she introduces me to Mr. Brent, an old white-whiskered man who she says is a direct descendant of one of the Founding Families. The town is named after his great-grandfather.

"I'm sorry about the prank," I whisper, when I shake his hand. But instead of giving me the stink eye, Mr. Brent smiles down at me.

"Don't fret," he says. "There's a solution for everything." Then he asks if I want to help him clean up the pond.

"Yes, of course," I say, and Mr. Brent waves for me to follow him.

He shows me how to use the little nets the community keeps in a bin beside the rock formation where I had posed Ava's doll Isabel a few days before. Following his instructions, I skim the top of the koi pond slowly, trying to get every last one of those tiny pellets, because Mr. Brent says the koi might swallow them and he's not sure what it could do to them.

I know what might happen, but I don't want to think about that. I don't want to think about how I almost killed the beautiful gold-and-white fish.

Looking around at the damage I've caused, how I've ruined the festivities and made all the kids in the neighborhood look at me like I'm some kind of jerk, makes me want to cry. But I fight back the tears and dump out a small batch of wet pellets, hitting the plastic handle against the lip of the bucket to make sure all the pellets fall out of it.

"Here," Ava says, coming up behind me to hand me my scope. "You're going to need this to look for pellets out there, on the other side of the street, because Mom says we have to get every last one of them."

I take my scope and put it around my neck.

"Thanks," I tell her.

"Don't thank me yet. We're going to be at this all day," Ava says, and she turns around and takes off before I can apologize for traumatizing Baxter, who is back in the house now, because Mom doesn't want him running around the neighborhood without a leash.

"Don't worry," Mr. Brent says. "We'll get this cleaned up in no time. See? We're almost done with the pond. And Harvey and his son are about to start up a new fire. We'll be sitting around, eating and having a good time, before you know it."

"I guess," I say as I glance over at all the families who are working together to clean up my mess. "It's nice of everyone to stay and help."

"That's what this community does best," Mr. Brent says. "We take care of each other—without complaints."

"I can see that," I say, because, to my surprise, every adult in the group is smiling and laughing and making the most of the job they are doing. "They don't look mad anymore."

"Of course not," Mr. Brent says. "We've all seen much worse than this."

"Worse?" I look up at Mr. Brent. His white eyebrows are very long, and the wind is playing with them, making them flap up and down. "I don't understand."

Mr. Brent wiggles his funny eyebrows and thinks. "Every one of the families on Pine Circle is a direct descendant of the Founding Families. People who came to Oregon for a fresh start way back when. In a sense, we've all grown up together, us, our children, and our children's children."

"Really?" I ask. "I didn't know that."

"Of course not. You just got here," Mr. Brent says, smiling

77

down at me. I look at the deep crinkles on his face and see something I recognize there. Compassion—my Ita used to have that, and I can see traces of it in Mr. Brent's blue eyes. "Moving's hard. I know. But, in the end, you'll see. It's all for the best."

"I hope so," I say as I skim the top of the koi pond again, getting fewer and fewer pellets with each stroke.

Mr. Brent knocks the pellets off his net. "It's a big sacrifice. Leaving everything you love and care for behind. Your family's very brave, James."

"I don't feel brave," I mumble under my breath before I can stop myself.

Mr. Brent laughs, a low, rumbling sound that makes his soft belly shake, and I think of Santa Claus, if the old Kringle were to shave his beard and lose the glasses.

"Oh, but you are, dear boy," Mr. Brent says. "Deep down inside, we're all braver than we think."

"Thanks." I smile, and Mr. Brent picks up the bucket and takes my net.

"Well, we're all done here. Thank you very much for all your help," he says. "Why don't you check on your mother, see what she needs help with next."

I leave the koi pond and go to my mother, who is standing with Mrs. Benson, Mrs. Coleman, and Stephanie's mother, Mrs. Johnson. They are keeping an eye on a rail-thin older man who is walking across the street, dragging an old red wagon full of trash behind him.

"Who's that?" I ask, when I see him peeking back at us as he leans over to pick up a piece of paper off the sidewalk.

But before anyone can answer me, a patrol car comes rolling up the bend and honks at him. The man stands up and stares back at the sheriff's vehicle. Then he turns and starts walking away, pulling the red wagon behind him like it doesn't weigh a thing, even though it's full to the top of its high wooden railing with all kinds of stuff he's picked up along the way.

"Oh, I wish Ben would leave him alone," Mrs. Benson says. "He's not harming anyone."

"Ben?" my mother asks.

"Sheriff Ben Michaels." Mrs. Benson's frown deepens, and she wrings her hands as she speaks. "I know he's just trying to do his job, but, really, I don't think this is necessary."

"Ms. Phillips called him," Mrs. Coleman says, pointing to a tall redheaded woman who is walking over to the patrol car.

Mrs. Benson gasps. "Dorothy? Why would she do that?"

Mrs. Johnson shrugs. "Maybe she thought it was her job. She is head of the homeowners' association."

I watch Mrs Phillips put her hands on the patrol car's door and lean over to talk to the sheriff inside. She shakes her head often, making her red curls bounce everywhere, as she talks. Finally, she steps back and stands on the curve of the street, watching the patrol car move slowly toward the older man.

Mrs. Benson sighs. "I know Mr. Morris hasn't been himself in a while, but he tries his best to be useful. He must have seen us picking up pellets and came over to help."

Mrs. Coleman smacks her lips. "Well, I know you think it's

harmless that he goes around picking up trash all day, but don't you think it's gotten out of hand?"

"It's been years," Mrs. Johnson whispers. "You'd think he'd pull himself together."

Mrs. Coleman shakes her head. "Last week, he stayed out all night with those dogs of his. Poor Betty was so worried about him."

My mother's eyebrows knit together on her forehead. Her lips are pressed tightly. And she looks uncomfortable.

"Well, let's not drag this out," she says as she hands me a plastic bag and starts walking with me to the play area beside the barbecue pit. "There's too much work to be done to stand around gawking."

I know what she's doing. My mother thinks the conversation sounds too much like chisme, and my mother doesn't like gossip. So, she's making sure we don't get caught up in it.

I start picking up the tiny little pellets clinging to the grass around the swing set. As I work, I keep peeking back to watch as the sheriff's car keeps rolling slowly up Pine Circle, following Mr. Morris until the strange man decides to cut across the grass and enter the tree line. The red wagon teeters this way and that, threatening to topple over as he disappears into the wall of Douglas firs.

Thanks to the people in the community, not just the kids and parents from our street but everyone else in the neighborhood, all the way down to Whitebark, the barbecue turns out to be a success. Though everyone's tired, and we all admit it's been a long day, the people on Pine Circle make sure we go home feeling happy about having moved here.

"That was good," my father says, when we get inside the house and head for the living room. "I'm glad they did that."

"Yes, well, you missed the bad part," Ava says, looking back at me resentfully. "James almost ruined everything."

I cringe, and my mother reaches for me. She pulls me in for a side hug. "Let's not go over that again," she says as she ruffles my hair and plants a kiss on the crown of my head.

"I said I was sorry," I mumble and look down at Baxter, who has come over to stand in the middle of his family circle.

"That's true," my father says. "I'm sure you learned your lesson. I'm just sorry I didn't see Baxter in this getup. I wonder if I would have recognized him."

"You wouldn't have," my mother says. "Even I was a little scared."

"Well, I'm glad it's ruined," Ava says. "I never want to see that spider costume on Baxter, ever again!"

"Not even for Halloween?" my father asks.

"Nope," Ava says, shaking her head. "Never means never."

Baxter barks at her, and we all laugh.

Much later, after I've showered, washed away the dirt and grime of all that work cleaning up, I come down for Family Movie Night.

Ava runs upstairs, changes into her purple pajamas, and my parents sort through their movie collection for something to watch. Then, with Baxter lying on the couch between me and Ava, we all sit around watching *The Wizard of Oz* because Ava absolutely refuses to let us watch *The Spider*, the black-and-white 1958 classic I suggest.

"Too soon?" my father asks when he puts it on the screen.

Ava nods. "Baxter needs time to recover."

CHAPTER 7

Ava walks ahead, ignoring me as we go up to bed, and I can't tell if it's because she's still upset by the prank or busy plotting her revenge. On Sunday morning, though, I find her playing outside.

Because she's so interested in science and nature, Ava leaves the backyard and walks over to the tree line behind our house. I follow her as she looks up at a flock of big black birds cawing and calling as they circle around overhead in the woods.

"What do you think they are?" Ava asks, when I come up and stand behind her. "Hawks?"

"I don't know, but whatever they are, they're definitely birds of prey," I say, picking up my scope and looking up at them. "Eagles, I think. No, wait. Vultures?"

"Oh! Let me see! Let me see!" Ava jumps up and down on the soles of her feet like she's five years old. I look at the dark silhouettes, mysterious and menacing against the gray sky, and hand over my scope.

Ava peers at the creatures and confirms my suspicions. "Yes. Vultures," she says. "Six of them."

"Seven," I correct her as we watch the birds make strange patterns in the sky as they start to move away. "Something's dead in these woods, and those nasty things want to get at it."

"Come on," Ava says. "Let's see where they're going."

"No thanks," I tell her.

Ava's eyes glitter with mischief. "Oooooooh . . . are you scared?"

"Aren't you?" I ask, listening to the black birds cawing loudly overhead.

"Don't be silly." Ava grins and squeals. "It's a sign!"

"It's not a sign," I tell her.

Then, because she never listens to anything I say, Ava starts to walk along the tree line. I walk behind her, looking at the birds through my scope as we go. We follow the black birds all the way down the neighborhood, moving slowly with them, because Ava wants to figure out what they are doing out here.

When we are so close we can see their feathers, Ava cups her hands around her lips and starts to let out a strange birdcall. I know what she's trying to do. This warbled cry is Ava's version of our Ita's screech owl call—the Lechuza's Song. The sound she used to bring to life the good witch owls in her stories of the antepasados.

Listening to Ava mimicking Ita's lechuzas, I can feel tears starting to burn in my eyes. But I don't want to cry. So, I push it all back and concentrate on what's in front of me.

Ava, and her messed-up version of our Ita's owl song.

"What are you doing?" I ask, looking around to make sure no one is watching her. "Stop it."

"Stop what?" she asks. "Calling out to them?"

"Yes," I say. "You're acting like a . . ."

"Acting like a what?" Ava puts a hand on her hip and stares at me the same way our mother stares when she thinks we're getting out of hand.

"Silly," I say. "You're acting silly."

"Oh, James," Ava laughs. "Don't you see? They're our ante-pasados, looking out for us."

Ava's a mystery sometimes. One minute, she's picking up specimens and talking about being a scientist, then she starts talking about magic. I can't tell if she really believes all those myths and legends Ita used to tell us when she put us to bed at night. I just know I don't.

"That's not a real call, Ava," I tell her. "It's just a silly thing Ita used to do. To entertain us, like all the other scary cuentos she told us. We were never meant to believe them. Not really."

"But I do believe them," Ava says.

"Then you're more gullible than I thought," I say. "Come on. Let's go home. I'm tired."

Suddenly, a feather falls from the sky. It floats slowly down, down, down, down, taking an eternity before it finally lands on the grass between us—a perfect, pale pluma with a sprig of soft, downy barbs at the base of it and a long, thin quill at the end. Mesmerized by the sight of the beautiful white feather, Ava bends down to pick it up.

"See?" Ava says, her wide eyes sparkling with awe. "The antepasados know you're scared. They heard you talking, and they want you to know we're not alone out here. This feather is their way of saying we shouldn't be afraid. I think we should go into the woods and find out why they're circling."

"It's a feather," I say flatly. "They fall off birds. There's nothing magical about that. And going into the woods is never a good idea. Come on, let's go home."

Then I take the stupid feather out of her hand and toss it aside.

Horrified, Ava jumps over and picks it up. "Don't do that!" she says, and she twirls it a few times in front of my face. Then she reaches over and tucks it into my shirt pocket, patting it down gently against my chest.

"A gift, then. From me to you," she says, and I nod, because that's what Ava does. Just when I think I know what she's up to, she surprises me by being super nice.

Satisfied, she turns around and we start heading home together. No pranking. No competition. Just me and my little sister, walking side by side—a white feather fluttering in my front shirt pocket.

We are almost home when we see an even stranger thing than those seven birds flying along the tree line. As we round the bend, we see that strange man, Mr. Morris, wrestling with two huge dogs in our driveway. He looks back at our trash can, sitting beside our bikes, as he pulls at their leashes.

"Can we help you?" I ask, my voice croaky and odd, because I'm super freaked-out. Mr. Morris turns to look at us. His weathered face is gaunt and, though he's not that old, his gray eyes are sunken deep into their sockets, and he looks surprised, like we're the last people on earth he'd expected to see out here.

"No!" he calls back as he leaves our driveway, walking quickly behind his two gangly chuchos. "I wasn't going through your trash. These two just can't stay out of people's flower beds."

"That's okay," Ava says. "Dogs will be dogs."

The man mumbles something fierce under his breath as he walks off, struggling to keep up with the long-legged beasts on their leashes.

"Who was that?" Ava asks.

"That's Mr. Morris," I tell her. "He goes around picking up trash."

"Oh, Stephanie told me all about him!" Ava says. "He lives down the street, with his daughter, Betty."

I look over at the trash can sitting on the side of the garage, next to our bikes, and something inside me tells me Mr. Morris is not telling the truth. Why else would he be hanging around our trash can if he wasn't thinking of picking through it? Just then, a strong wind rushes up to us. It sweeps up the fallen leaves and debris in our street and swirls it all around us.

The strange wind presses against us, pulling at our clothes and pushing at our chests. Leaves swirl up and come rolling toward us, bringing with them all kinds of fragments. Papers and wrappers and tiny twigs that roll and roil, coming at us like a relentless storm that won't be contained.

Ava turns away from it. Her hair swirls across her face and she tries to pull it together in her fist. I put my arms up and try to keep the wind from throwing debris into my eyes. Then, as suddenly as it came, the wind is gone. Nothing but silence surrounds us—a dense, scary silence that makes me lower my arms and look at Ava, who turns and stares at the muted world around us.

"Whoa!" Ava exclaims. "Did you see that dirt devil?"

As all kinds of rubble settle around us, I look up. The sky above is turning a deep, marbled gray, and I can smell moisture in the air. Behind us, the garage door suddenly opens.

"Jaimito! Ava!" our father calls from inside the garage. "Get your bikes in here. It's about to rain."

"Okay!" I yell over my shoulder. "Come on, Ava. Let's go."

Ava runs up the driveway with me and we reach our bikes at the same exact time. She grabs the handles on hers and I grab mine. I am about to move it, when I notice something caught in the spokes. A piece of paper. A familiar shape. A familiar size.

Another envelope!

Another prank!

But it can't be a prank, because Ava has been with me all morning. Unless, of course . . . No, she couldn't have. She hasn't had time. Has she? But if it wasn't her . . . then, that means . . .

"What is that?" Ava asks when she sees me pull it out from between the spokes.

I turn it over and read the familiar inscription. "A letter."

An eerie silence comes over us as we lean over and read the long, elegant script.

~~James Anthony McNichols~~

"Was this here . . . before?" I ask my sister.

Because I am suddenly scared, my heart is racing, and I am shaking like one of those leaves caught in the windstorm a few seconds ago. So, I take a deep breath and let it out slowly.

"I don't know," Ava says. "I didn't see it before."

I turn the letter over in my hands and stare at the wax seal on the back. Ava moves to stand close beside me. "Who's it from?" she asks, and her wide, innocent eyes tell me she's not behind this.

I look down the road, at the figure of Mr. Morris getting smaller and smaller as he makes his way home. "I'm not sure."

Ava's eyes widen. "Well? Are you going to open it?"

"Yes," I say. Then, because I can't deal with this right now, I fold the letter and shove it in my back pocket. "I'll read it later. When we get inside."

I grab my bike and walk it into the garage.

"We," Ava says. "We'll open it later."

Something about the way Ava says that, with so much interest and enthusiasm, makes me wonder if I've got this all wrong and she's just pulled the best prank ever. Confused, I rush into the house and run up to my room. Because there's no lock on my door, there's no way of keeping Ava out of my space. But that's okay, because I want to see her reaction when I open the letter. To be honest, I'd much rather this be a prank than think that someone really is watching everything I do up here.

Ava stands around waiting while I put my scope on the corner of my desk chair and take off my rain jacket and hang it up. But she scoots in beside me when I take out the letter, put my finger under the flap, and give it a good tug. The seal snaps off, and I open it slowly.

Dear James,

Did you forget I'm watching you? Why did you throw my letter away? What's the matter? Are you afraid?

That's too bad. I thought you might prove to be more courageous—I thought you might want to protect your family, to keep them safe in this house. I hope you know, you don't have time to waste.

The Blood Moon is almost upon us. If you don't act before the sun covers the moon's face, you put everyone and everything in danger. Time *to make something happen. And remember, I'm still watching you!*

The Keeper

"The Blood Moon?!" Ava's high-pitched voice tells me she's just as creeped out by the letter as I am, which destroys my whole theory. Unless, of course, she's faking it.

"Okay, you can stop now," I say. "This outdoes any prank I've ever played on you. You got me. I was scared."

"What?" Ava looks confused.

I roll my eyes. "Come on . . . How did you do it? How did you make this look so legit?"

Ava puts a hand on her chest. "Me? Make that? Why would I do that?"

"Ah, hello! To get me back for your dolls, and for Spiderdog!" I say.

"James!" Ava takes the letter out of my hand and inspects it carefully. "I didn't write this!"

"Yes, you did," I say. "Just admit it. How long have you been planning this prank?"

"I didn't do this!" Ava slaps my arm with the letter. "I don't have fancy paper. And what kind of glue is this? I've never seen weird glue like this before!"

"You have to stop," I say, taking the letter from her and folding it back up. "Mom and Dad are sick of our pranks."

"Why won't you believe me?" Ava crosses her arms in front

of her and turns to stare at the door.

Ignoring her, I look at the letter in my hand. "But if you didn't write this . . . then that means . . ."

"Someone else did it," Ava says. "Some creepy person, like that Mr. Morris!"

I think back to what Mrs. Benson said at the barbecue. "No, he's not a bad person," I tell her. "He's just not . . . Mrs. Benson would have told us if he was a bad person. I think."

"I don't know," Ava says. "He was standing right there, by our bikes, when we got here. I don't think he was looking at the trash can. I think he was looking back at the bikes. He wanted to make sure he put it on the right one!"

"Something isn't right here," I say, trying to figure out if Ava is trying to throw me off her trail. "This doesn't make sense, Ava. Why would Mr. Morris be watching me?"

"I don't know." Ava stares at the envelope in my hand.

"Do you think . . . could this mean . . . do we have—*a stalker*?"

Ava's eyes widen. She looks horrified. But only for a moment, because then she narrows her eyes and glares at me. "Wait a minute . . . are you pranking me again? That's not fair, James. I didn't get you back for what you did to Baxter!"

"What? No, Ava." I wave the letter in front of her. "This is real."

"Stop it!" Ava yells. She sprints across the room and opens the door to leave. "This isn't funny, James. I'm not playing any-more."

CHAPTER 8

That evening, after a series of texts with Beto and Mike, I sit inside my hanging tent because, honestly, I feel safer hiding inside the cocoon of blue fabric than I do sitting on my bed. In here, nobody can see me.

I twirl the white feather in my hand and wonder what Ita would say about it. Would she dismiss it, the way I did when it landed in front of me, or would she say it means something, the way Ava did?

I push my hand out of my tent and reach out to set the feather on my nightstand. Because I'm still pretty freaked-out and I want to get my mind off those creepy letters, I open up my phone to my videos and start going through my collection of "Consejos From the Other Side," the title Ita gave to the videos I took of her in the hospital on my phone. I know there's a video in there where Ita talks about signs.

Because she was getting weaker and she didn't dress up, Ita

is wearing a white hospital gown in this video. But her hair is up and her dangly crystal earrings hang so low, they brush her thin shoulders. Her smile is weak, but her brown eyes are bright as ambers as she looks into the camera and says, *"Look for signs from me, cariño. Wherever you go, watch for feathers and rainbows and pretty rocks. When you find them, you'll know I'm around."*

Then she lifts the moonstone owl pendant she always wears around her neck and shakes it in front of my phone camera. *"There are signs everywhere, my love."* Looking at her brings a hot rush of tears to my eyes, and I shut the phone off quickly.

"Ridiculous! There's no signs. No magic . . ."

The words leave my lips before I can stop them, and I shove the phone back into my pocket and spin my tent around so that it makes a soothing movement that helps me relax. There's no way I can show Ava that video. Nope. She couldn't handle it. It would make her cry again. I'm sure of it. Suddenly, the curtain flips open and Ava says, "Just tell me the truth. Were you pranking me again?"

"I was not," I tell her. "I promise."

"I didn't think so." Ava crawls into my hanging tent with me. "Not after the mess you made yesterday."

"What are you doing?!" I ask, pulling the buds out of my ears quickly. "You can't be in here. You're getting too big to crawl in with me."

"Uh-uh." Ava shakes her head. "I'm not too big. The thing

holds over two hundred pounds. I know, I read the instructions when Dad put it together."

"Still," I say, squirming around, trying my best to show her how uncomfortable I am with her in here. "This is my personal space. For my personal time."

"You're watching videos of Ita, aren't you?" Ava lies back beside me and puts my happy face pillow behind her head.

I want to lie, to say, *"No. Now get out of here and leave me alone,"* but I don't. Because it suddenly hits me—*Ava is missing Ita as much as I am!* Of course, that explains why she was so attached to that feather. Why didn't I realize that before?

The truth is, I feel bad that I'm the only one who can listen to Ita's consejos anytime I want. It's not Ava's fault that Ita put me in charge of them, that she made me promise to keep them on my phone and only share these new ones, the ones we filmed at the hospital, with Ava when she is ready—when she is older and has gotten over Ita's passing.

Ava stares, makes ojitos at me, and I look away. "Can I see her? she pleads. "Just one video. Please. I haven't asked in a long time. Not even once since we got here."

"I don't know," I say. "I don't want to make you—"

Ava stops me. "I won't cry, if that's what you're worried about."

I think about it. I don't know what I'm going to do if she cries. I just finished crying myself, so how can I expect her not to do it? She's younger than me. I sigh and hand her an earbud. "Okay, but you can't talk during the video."

"No forwarding. No pausing. No chatting." Ava recites the three golden rules of watching videos with me. She shifts around, pushes the earbud into her ear, and settles into position.

I open my video gallery and start scrolling down, reading the titles as I go, concentrating on the funny videos, for obvious reasons. "'Relámpago Rats'? 'Cheetahs Chismosas'? 'Crafty Cucarachas'..."

"You pick," Ava says, resting her head on my shoulder. "They're all good."

I click on "Moldy Muñecas" because it's pretty cute the way the filthy dolls jump in the washing machine just so they can sit down to eat at the table with the family at the end, plus it's one of her favorites. But we don't stop there. Because she's taking it well, Ava and I sit inside my tent for almost an hour watching video after video. We listen to our Ita's kooky, wild stories until we've laughed so much, our stomachs hurt.

"Just one more," Ava begs. "A short one."

"Okay, you pick," I say, handing her the phone.

Ava scrolls up and down. Her finger lingers on the last video I recorded of our Ita. In the video, our grandmother's long silver hair is almost all gone, and she looks a little frail, thin and gaunt in her white hospital gown.

"Can I?" Ava whispers, her finger hovering over the video.

I nod, and Ava presses play.

On the screen, Ita sits up in bed. The light from her window filters in and shines all around her. She looks like an angel, staring out at the beautiful, sunlit world. *"Okay,"* I say, from behind the camera. *"You're on."*

"Last one, Jaimito," Ita whispers, smiling softly into the camera. *"Soon, I will be with the antepasados. Watching over you from the other side."*

You can't see me in the video, but you can hear me say *"I love you,"* quietly, because I didn't want to show her how much it hurt me to hear her talk about leaving. Even though I know she was trying to make sure I knew we were all going to be okay afterward.

"Don't be sad." Ita's warm brown eyes glisten with love. *"Move joyfully in this world, cariño. Love your family. Love them with all your heart. Remember, your sister is clever and you are courageous, but together you can overcome any obstacle. And above all else, brave boy, remember that nobody has the right to tell you where and how to live. Nobody has the right to take your dreams away from you. Stand tall. Stand together."*

"Nobody," Ava whispers, wiping away a tear as the video ends and I turn off the phone.

Listening to her repeat that word sends a chill over my entire body, and suddenly I understand.

"That's it!" I say, sitting up straight, accidentally ripping the earbud out of Ava's ear.

"Ouch!" Ava cries. "That hurt! What's the matter with you?"

"Don't you see?" I ask her, rolling up my earbuds and pushing them into my pants pocket with my phone. "That's what's

97

going on. . . . the Keeper's trying to scare us away. This whole time, while the rest of the neighborhood was welcoming us, he's been trying to run us off."

"Run us off?" Ava whispers, her eyes wide and bright. "But why?"

"I don't know. Because we're different," I speculate.

Ava frowns. "You mean, because we're . . . Mexican." She says the word without flinching. She's only ten years old, but because of all the work our mother does with diversity, we are very familiar with this topic. "So, they're racists?"

"Prejudiced, or biased," I correct her. "Maybe. I don't know. The point is, all this time the Keeper's been making it very clear we don't belong. It's like he's challenging us to fit in, to make a life out here, in their world, without our loved ones to help us!"

"I don't get it," Ava says, making the fabric tent swirl around as she scrambles to sit up. "What do you mean 'all this time'?"

"You haven't read the first letter," I say. "But it makes sense, when you put the two letters together."

I push the curtain back.

"Wait, there's another letter?" Ava asks as we climb out of the tent.

It twirls around behind us, and I walk over to the desk. I dig the Keeper's first letter out of my drawer, because I just couldn't leave it in the trash can, not after that second letter arrived. I open it and compare them. Ava stands beside me and reads both letters aloud, one right after the other.

"James . . . this is serious," she says, her eyes shining brightly with something like fear in them.

"I know," I tell her. "We have to figure out who's sending these."

"How are we going to do that?" Ava plops herself down on the corner of my bed. "Where do we start? I mean, if you don't think Mr. Morris is doing it, then who else?"

"I don't know," I tell her. "But we don't have much time. It says here the Blood Moon is approaching. Whatever that is."

"It's an eclipse," Ava says. "The next one is in five days. I know, I like to keep up with them."

"Wow!" I say. "That doesn't give us much time."

Ava nods. "You know what else is in five days?" And when I give her a blank stare, she says, "Mom's New Faculty Gala."

"Faculty Gala?"

"Uh-huh. It's on the calendar for Friday," Ava says. "But it doesn't matter. This is more important. We have to figure out what the Keeper wants," she says. "If we knew that, we'd have something to go by. You know, like on that show on TV about unsolved mysteries."

I read through the first letter again. "I get the feeling this has something to do with the house. He keeps saying . . . Oh my God!"

"What?" Ava jumps up and looks at the letter quivering in my hand.

I look around the room, put my hand over my lips, and

whisper low enough so that only she can hear me. "What if there's hidden cameras in here?"

Ava's head stays still as she moves her eyes sideways and up into the corners, to look around the room without giving herself away. "Seriously?"

"That's it. We have to show Mom and Dad the letters," I say. "I mean . . . that's if . . ."

"What?" Ava asks.

"Ava, are you telling me the truth?" I ask her. "Can you swear you didn't write these?"

"James!" Ava raises her arms in the air and sighs. "If I really did do it, and you fell for it, why would I lie about it now?"

I shrug my shoulders. "I dunno."

Ava leans over and offers me her pinkie finger. "I honest-to-goodness, double-dutch, enchilada-rush, pinkie-swear, on my dolls' cute hair, that I did not write these letters."

Even though it feels a bit silly to do it, I lean over and join pinkies with Ava.

"Okay then. Let's do this," I say, and then I walk out of my room.

With the letters in my hand, Ava and I race each other down the stairs and run into the kitchen. My father is standing over the stove with an oven mitt on one hand and a spatula in the other.

"Well, hello," he says. "It's about time you two came down. Ready for some hot cheesy goodness?"

My mother drops a fork. It clatters on the plate at the foot of the table and she reaches down and moves it so that it's in its proper place. "What you got there, Jaimito?"

"Mom, Dad," Ava starts. "James has something important to tell you."

"I think you should read these." I raise my arm to show my parents the strange letters.

"What's this?" my mother asks, putting down the silverware and taking the letters from me.

"I don't really know," I say as I watch her unfold and read them. "Some kind of creepy notes."

My father puts the spatula down and comes to read over my mother's shoulder.

"What do you mean you don't know?" my mother asks. "Where did you get these?"

"The first one was sitting up against my computer when I got home on Thursday, and the second one was stuck between the spokes of my bike this afternoon," I tell her.

Then I go ahead and describe the incidents how crooped out I've been but also how Ava says she has nothing to do with it. Our parents listen and stare back and forth at each other as I lay it all out for them.

"James!" my father exclaims, smiling broadly. And he takes the letters from my mother and examines the strange seals. "I'm impressed. Where'd you get the wax for this?"

Perplexed, I blink.

Then I look at my mother, but she is shaking her head and smiling at me too.

"That's a good one, James," she says. "You really had me going for a moment there!"

"What?" I ask. "This isn't a joke! Someone came into the house and left that letter in my room. They're out there right now, watching us!"

"Really?" my father asks. Then he looks out the wide dining room window and shares a secret smile with our mother. "Hmm. Should we ask them to join us for dinner? What do you think, mi amor? Do we have enough for one more?"

"Stop it!" Ava screams. "This isn't funny! James is . . . James is . . ."

"Pulling a fast one!" my father says, and he turns around and goes back to the kitchen because the oven has started beeping. "Oh, my casserole's ready!"

"Mom. Dad. I know this looks like one of our pranks, but you have to believe us," I beg. "We didn't do this. This is real. Someone in this neighborhood is stalking us!"

"¡Uy! You think they can hear us?" My mother raises her hands in front of her and makes spooky, wavy fingers toward Ava. "Maybe we should close the curtains, so the Cucuy can't get us."

My sister throws her arms up in the air and then brings them down fast, slapping them against her pants loudly. My mother leans back, surprised. "Okay," she says. "That's enough scary stuff for one night. Let's just eat. I'm starving."

"Are you sure we can't invite the Keeper?" my father asks me, setting his casserole on the table in front of my mother. "Ooooooh. Maybe he can bring a friend! I wonder if he knows the Creature from the Black Lagoon?"

"Dad!" Ava whines. "Stop it. This is important."

"Okay. Fine." My mother rolls her eyes in an exaggerated way. "I'll make a salad—then we'll have enough."

I look at the letters sitting on the table next to my mother and pull them toward me. "Thanks!" I say sarcastically, folding the letters and putting them in my back pocket. "Thank you for believing us!"

My father gives me a side-eyed glance. "Well, what did you expect, son?" he asks. "After the last few days, I think it's safe to say your mother and I are not going to get sucked into your little prank war anymore."

"You two are just going to have to figure out this pranking business by yourselves," my mother chimes in. "That's it for us. We're through with this nonsense."

That's the thing about being a prankster—nobody ever takes you seriously, especially when you're done playing games.

I don't want to be mad about it.

But I am.

CHAPTER 9

"You know what this means, don't you?" Ava tells me as we walk up the stairs side by side at bedtime with Baxter in front of us.

"We're going to have to figure this out by ourselves," I whisper, because I don't want our parents or whoever else can hear us to know what we're talking about.

Ava leans over. "So, who do you think is sending those letters?"

I shrug. "I'm not sure. Everybody here's so nice. Mrs. Benson, Mr. Brent, all the parents, they all really try to take care of each other. I mean, you saw how the whole neighborhood pulled together to clean up my mess yesterday, and they weren't even mad about it. Even Mr. Morris was trying to help."

"I still think there's something there," Ava mumbles. "Can we at least not cross him off the list yet?"

"What list?" I ask.

"The list we should start," Ava says. "We need to keep our eyes peeled from now on and start putting together a list of suspects."

"That's a good idea," I tell her. "But first we have to find whatever device they're using to *'watch'* me. I know we only have five days to figure this out, but I want to make sure they can't see or hear us while we're doing it."

"For sure. Can we start tonight?" Ava asks. "After Mom and Dad go to bed?"

Downstairs, the TV goes silent and I can hear my parents talking to each other, so I know they're getting ready to settle in for the night.

"No." I shake my head. "Tomorrow morning, when we can see better. I don't want to sneak around in the dark. We might miss something."

"Good point." Ava nods.

"What are you two up to now?" my father asks as he and our mother start coming up the stairs.

"Nothing," I say. "We were just saying good night."

My father climbs the last stair and steps around so that he and my mother are standing between me and Ava.

"Well, good night, you two," he says, and he gives each of us a hug. Then he leans over and ruffles Baxter's fur. "Good night, Spiderdog."

"Dad! Don't call him that," Ava cries. "I don't want it to stick."

"Okay, all right," my father says, and he heads to their room.

"Good night, my little lagartijos!" My mother cups my face with her hands and gives me loud kisses all over my cheeks and temples and forehead. Then she does the same to Ava before she pushes us gently toward our rooms on the opposite side of the house from the master bedroom.

I try to go to bed, but my mind keeps going over and over the Keeper's letters, and I just can't sleep. Frustrated, I toss my colcha aside and sit up. Looking at my window, I realize I can't go out there. What if he's watching me right this minute?

Looking around my room, I decide not to wait till the morning to start looking for hidden cameras. I check behind the curtains, go through things on the shelves above my desk, I even stand on my desk chair and peek into the air-conditioning vent, but I don't find anything.

However, things change when I go through my closet. When I look up at the things on the top shelf, I notice something I hadn't seen before. There's some kind of door up there. *Could that go up to the attic? I thought the attic hatch was in the hallway. So, what does this little door lead to?* I wonder.

I stand on my chair again and move my box of comics to the side so I can reach up there, but when I try to push it open, it won't give. I push on it several more times, but it's stuck, glued down by old paint. *Who would paint over an attic door?* This is too suspicious! And even though my heart is pounding furiously inside my chest and my palms are starting to sweat, I can't let fear stop me.

I have to know what's up there!

I take my hockey stick and poke at it, trying to pry the little door away from the paint quietly so that I don't wake up my parents. Dust particles fall off it, and I poke it again, harder this time. It creaks. More dust falls off. Only this time, the lid gives. I poke at it over and over again, until the door pops open, swinging back and forth before it stays still. I stare at the darkness on the other side of it.

The crawl space is pretty tight, but I manage to get myself through it. Crouched down, I use the flashlight feature on my phone to scan the attic space. The room is dark and, even with the flashlight, I can't see very far, but I do spot a small window. Of course! I've seen the small window before, from outside, but I never questioned where it might be in the house.

I open the window and let the moonlight in, but it doesn't help much. Looking around, I see a couple of old cobwebs hanging from the corners of the rafters above me and a few dusty half-torn boxes. *Why do people leave their old stuff behind?* I wonder as I poke at the tired boxes and lift the tattered lids with my hockey stick.

Because I don't want to miss anything, I go through every box. Books. Filthy clothes. Broken toys. A tin box with yellowed dominoes. Playing cards. Junk, mostly. Disappointed that I don't find any cameras up there, I decide to climb down. I make it a point to secure the access door before I close the closet.

Though I try to get some rest, I spend most of the night tossing and turning in a fitful sleep so that when I finally wake up, I am a mess. My hair is standing up more than usual and my eyes feel puffy, but I know I have to get up. I can smell something delicious wafting up the stairs.

"Are they gone?" I ask Ava, because she is eating by herself at the breakfast nook with Baxter at her feet.

"Yup!" Ava nods as she shoves a forkful of pancakes into her mouth, chews, and swallows it down quickly. "Mom had to go in early for some kind of meeting."

"Good," I say, pulling the plate of pancakes my parents left on the counter toward me.

Ava shoves the last bite of pancake into her mouth and chews it quickly. "Okay. I'm ready to start whenever you are."

"I figure we should start upstairs. I already checked out my room last night."

"You didn't find anything?" Ava asks as she watches me tear through my breakfast.

"No," I say, swallowing down a big bite of my pancakes. "Well, I did find a secret door in my closet."

Ava's eyes light up and she sits up straight. "A secret door?!"

"It leads to a small room up in the attic," I tell her. "But there's nothing in there. Just a lot of old junk—trash, mostly."

"I checked my room too," Ava says. "This morning, when I could see everything, but I didn't find anything."

Ava puts her plate in the sink and she and Baxter follow me upstairs. We go through our parents' room, the linen closet, my mother's office, and the hall bathroom, but there are no signs of hidden cameras anywhere.

Downstairs, the living room and kitchen look fine, and we look around the foyer and end up in the den. It's the biggest room in the house. My father's computer desk and his work materials are all on the far-left wall, and Ava and Baxter go around looking through every nook and cranny of that area.

I check out the big bookcase full of his books behind my father's desk, but I don't find anything, so I go over to one end of the huge den. I shift the flowers around the centerpiece on the side table and even look under the large game table where we play cards and checkers on Family Game Nights.

"Nothing here," Ava says, and she and Baxter walk to the other end of the den going over every window along the wall.

Baxter gets tired of sleuthing and jumps up on the couch, while I check out the massive coffee table, the love seat, and the two leather wingback chairs that sit in front of him. And when I am done, we sit together on the couch and stare at the other two matching built-in bookshelves that run all the way up to the ceiling. There are old-fashioned rolling ladders that make reaching for a book an adventure. The thought of going through all those books gives me a headache. I flop on my side, so that I'm halfway lying on the couch with my head next to Baxter's.

"What are we going to do?" Ava asks. "This room is huge!"

"We have to take it one section at a time," I tell her. "Check every little thing. We can't afford to miss anything."

I glance at the giant centerpiece's copper tray with its long, swooping glass container full of potpourri. The scent coming from it is soothing, some kind of flower-and-spice combination that reminds me of Thanksgiving.

But when my eyes scan the floor and I see the edge of the

109

thick carpet that keeps the iron legs of the table from scratching the floor, I sit up with a jerk.

"What?" Ava asks when she sees me staring at the floor in front of us.

I put my index finger up against my lips and hush her. "Shhh . . ." Then I point at the corner of the carpet, where I see that the tiles don't quite touch together. The gap between the tiles is thin, but it forms a straight line about three feet long.

Ava jumps up.

Together, we push the massive wooden table off the carpet. Baxter circles us, whining and whimpering and wagging his tail. And when we pull back the carpet, there it is! A trap door—built into the floor. We walk around it, staring at the mysterious door, a three-by-three square piece of floor that looks like a perfect cutout dropped back into place. Because there are no hinges, no lock, no handle, nothing to let us open it, I scratch my head and look up at Ava.

"Well, that's weird," I say. "How do we open it?"

"Maybe," Ava whispers, "there is some kind of secret handle in the room. You know, like in the movies, when someone pulls on a book on the shelf in an old library . . ."

"You watch too much TV," I say. "It can't be that simple."

"But what if it is?" Ava says. "What if the Keeper has some kind of control room down there? What if he's got all kinds of monitors he looks into?"

To make her point, Ava walks over to the bookshelf and

starts looking at the old fancy-looking books that came with the house. "I would think it would be the oldest, most uninteresting book . . ."

I consider the iron tools in the fireplace stand. Could I use one of them as a crowbar? I don't want to damage the floorboards, so I stand there and stare at the trap door. Then, because I don't know what else to do, I press down on the corner of the trap door with the sole of my shoe.

Immediately, I feel a small amount of give in the floor, and the lid creaks and lifts just a tiny bit. Baxter goes crazy, sniffing and snorting around the crack.

"Get back, boy," I tell him. When I take my foot off the corner, the floorboard closes again, leaving a line of unsettled dust along the edges of the door.

"Ava!" I whisper, a hushed excitement in my voice. "Ava! Look!"

When she turns around, I do it again. I press the sole of my foot on the corner, harder this time, and the floorboard creaks and lifts again. Ava's eyes widen. She holds Baxter back and stares as the trap door closes with a heavy sigh, puffing out more dust as it shuts.

"Holy macaroni!" she says. "Do it again. Wait. I'll see if I can keep it open."

"Use a fire poker," I say. "The one that looks like a spatula."

Ava grabs the iron tool out of the fireplace stand and waits, feet shoulder-width apart, in front of the trap door. Baxter sits

111

back in front of the fireplace and watches us.

I position myself better and press down on the middle seam of the trap door, putting the whole of my weight on my foot. The door lifts higher than before, and Ava shoves the iron spatula in so that it doesn't close on us again.

Shaking with excitement, I walk around and lift the door.

"Ah, there it is. You see that?" I show Ava a little wooden arm tucked into the left side of the seam. Then I pull the arm out and anchor it down so that the door stays open. I take the phone out of my pocket and use the flashlight to shine light into the opening.

"Stay," I tell Baxter as I start to ease myself down into the secret space under the door. Baxter sits back and groans, because he knows I mean it.

"Yes. Stay," Ava warns him as she follows me down.

The stairs look moldy, and I smell must and mildew and some kind of rodent poison drifting up into the den, but I start to go down the creaky, cranky stairs to the basement anyway. The air is thick. We can see dust particles floating and dancing in the light coming from my phone.

Halfway down the stairs, Ava finds a light switch. When she turns it on, the bare lightbulb hanging from the ceiling is pretty dim, and I look around at the place in horror. Absolutely everything is covered in a thick gray blanket of dust.

"How old is this stuff?" Ava asks. "It looks like Dracula's lair down here."

"You watch too many old movies," I say. Though, secretly, I can't help but agree with her.

The place looks like a dungeon. The walls are made of rock, and the few pieces of furniture in the room look like they're ready for the trash. I walk by a scratched-up table with a ripped tassel lamp and a ragged tablecloth. Another table with broken dishes and chipped cups sits tipped against a wall.

A pile of torn, tattered magazines lays on a nightstand, and the upholstery on a set of dining room chairs is ripped and worn. Absolutely everything is covered in that filthy gray dust that makes us cough and cover our faces with our shirts.

"Whoa!" Ava exclaims as we stand in the middle of the basement. "This is unbelievable! You think Mom and Dad know about this? I mean, was a basement even in the Realtor's description?"

I touch the top of the table and a film of dust comes off on my fingertips. And when I push down and put some weight against it, to test its sturdiness, the whole table wobbles.

"I doubt it," I say, wiping my hands on my pants. "These things are falling apart."

I walk over to a bookshelf and peek into one of the boxes sitting on it while Ava goes through the gadgets in a wooden toolbox. "So, what exactly are we looking for?" she asks. "Because I don't see any new technologies being used down here. This is just a lot of old junk."

"I'm not sure. I'll know it when I see it," I say as I zero in on a tall, heavy-looking box sitting high up on a shelf. I squint and read the label. *Personal*, I think it reads, but I can't be sure, because the letters are faded. I want to pull it down but it's way up there.

Suddenly, we hear a loud pop. *Snap, crackle, fizz!* The light goes out, and Ava screams.

"Ahhhh! What was that?" she asks.

My heart thumps wildly against my chest and my pulse throbs in my ears. I let out a stuttering breath and press my fist against my breastbone, massaging the susto away. Everything about this is creeping me out, but I can't let Ava know that. I don't want to scare her.

"The bulb burned out," I say, and I pull my phone out of my pocket and use the flashlight to find my sister in the dark. "You okay?"

"Yes, I'm fine now," she says. "It was just . . . Never mind. I'm okay now."

I lay my phone facedown on the wobbly table so that the flashlight can act as a lightbulb for now. Ava snakes her way around to the table. She looks through a box sitting on one of the chairs.

Wham!

The sound of the trap door slamming shut makes us jump, and Ava and I stare at each other in the dimness of the basement without saying a word. For a moment, we look like two wax figures, motionless, eyes shining in the dark.

"We can get out, right?" Ava's voice, when she finally speaks, is as squeaky and tiny as a mouse's. She stands very still, her wide eyes glistening. "Tell me we can get out."

I nod and put my finger over my lips.

Kruuuuuppf... kruuuuumpt... kruuuuumpt...

"What is that?" Ava squeaks.

"I don't know," I whisper. And I put my hand on Ava's shoulder to let her know it's going to be okay because I'm right here with her. "Baxter? Is that you, boy?"

We wait. But when nothing else happens, when the noise doesn't come back, I let out a deep breath and smile at my sister. "Just old house noises," I say. "Ita used to say every house has them."

"That was too creepy," Ava whispers.

"¿Cucuy?" I ask her.

"Definitely Cucuy," Ava says, wringing her hands and looking around the dark room.

"You wanna go back up?" I ask quietly, but she shakes her head.

I give her my phone, so she can feel more in control.

I really don't want to go back up either. I want to see what's inside that box. The line from the Keeper's first letter, *Your house is very special... explore it, try to uncover its many secrets,* has crept into my mind, and now it's going around and around in my head. So, I really want to find out what the Keeper was talking about.

I can't be sure until I get it down, but I have a feeling that box is storing important documents. *Personal* means it might have someone's diary or journal. What kind of secret is the guardian of this house keeping?

Because the box is so high up, I pull several big books off the shelf and build a stack on the ground. I'm stepping onto them, to reach the box, when I hear something. A soft shuffle, quiet footsteps, are getting closer and closer. I freeze and listen. But I don't have time to do much else, because suddenly I hear a horrible loud noise coming from behind the shelf.

KREEEEEEEEN!

The shelf moves, shifts, and falls—with me clinging to the wooden boards like a feral cat.

Whooooomp!

Before I can do anything to stop it, the bookshelf topples over and collapses, falling over me in a great big tidal wave of books and bulky boxes. I jump, arms outstretched, and dive to the ground.

"Jaaaaames!" Ava screams.

The top of the bookshelf lands with a hard thud on the old table, where it teeters and sways side to side. The basement is in complete darkness because Ava dropped my phone to run across the room. It's lying facedown where neither of us can reach it, but at least we're not in the dark. Forsaking the phone, Ava pulls on my arm to help me scoot away from the rubble, and I crawl out from under the blanket of books and boxes.

"Are you okay?" she asks. I can hear the panic in her voice as she touches my arms and shoulders and head.

"I'm fine. I'm fine." I sit there for a moment, coughing, as I dust myself off.

Ava runs and gets my phone. My arm hurts, but I don't want to make a big fuss and scare my sister.

"Can you walk?" Ava asks, and I test my legs.

My left knee hurts and my right ankle might be sprained. "Yes. I'm fine."

When we open the trap door and crawl back out, Baxter won't let us through. He's so happy to see us, he can't stop wagging his tail and licking our faces. "Down, boy," I tell him as I limp over to the love seat and ease myself down into it.

"How's your arm?" Ava asks when she sees me pulling it against my chest, like a broken bird wing.

"Please don't fuss," I say. "Nothing's wrong with me."

"Let me see. Can you move your hand? How about your leg?" Ava asks as she inspects me thoroughly. "You didn't hit your head, did you? You're not dizzy. Are you dizzy?"

"I got up here, didn't I?" I insist. "Nothing's broken. I'm not dizzy. Everything's fine, I promise."

Ava's eyes glisten as she looks down at me. Then she starts dusting us off, because we are both covered in filth.

I glance sideways over at Baxter and ruffle and tug at his fur. "You weren't scared, were you, boy?" I ask. "Because there's nothing to be scared of. I wouldn't let anything happen to you or Ava."

Ava sits next to me and smiles weakly. "Why don't you lie down in the living room," she suggests. "I'll put on your favorite movie and makes us some cocoa. Real cocoa. Without salt, and lots of sugar."

"That sounds good," I say, giving her what I hope is a reassuring grin. "I need some sugar to soothe away the susto."

Ava laughs. "That's what Ita used to say, remember?" she asks. "When she used to spook us?"

I nod and grin at her. "To keep us on our toes."

Once I'm settled on the couch, with a mountain of cushions around me and Baxter's head resting on my lap, Ava brings me my steaming cup of chocolate de olla.

"Let me look at your head," she says when I put down my cocoa on the coffee table. "Is that a welt? I think that's a welt on your forehead."

"It's dirt," I say, after I wipe the stain off with my fingertips. I touch a scrape on my right elbow, where the skin is a little tender, and wince. "Other than some scuffs and scrapes, I think I'm all right."

"I'll go get the first aid kit," Ava says, and she runs up to the master bathroom. When she gets back, she's got the first aid kit in one hand and she's dragging our colchas behind her. "I thought you might want to take a nap later."

"Do you think it's weird?" I ask her while she puts ointment on my elbow. "How that bookcase just fell forward like that?"

"What do you mean?" Ava asks.

"Well, there was no reason for it to fall over," I explain.

"Unless someone pushed it over. I mean, it was dark. And I couldn't see anything. Could you see anything?"

"No," Ava admits.

"Then there were those creaky, creepy noises," I remind her. "And that great big wallop. Just before the whole thing came toppling over."

Ava's eyes widen. "You think *someone* was down there with us?"

"I'm not so sure, but I think I heard footsteps. So, yeah, maybe . . . maybe *someone* or *something* pushed that bookshelf over." I stop, because I can see that this is making Ava nervous.

Ava's lips tremble a little, then she shakes her head. "I think it was just a door slamming too hard."

"What door?" I ask her.

"I don't know," she whispers. "The front door?"

"Why would the front door slam?" I ask, because I want to get to the bottom of what really happened down in the basement. "No one was here to slam it."

Ava thinks again. "The pantry door sticks," she says. "I noticed that the first day we moved in here."

"Same. Same," I tell her. "No one here to open it."

"Was that you in the pantry, boy?" Ava asks Baxter. Baxter opens his eyes. He wags his tail once, and then he closes his eyes again. Ava sighs and throws her colcha over her legs. Then she pulls it over her arms and shoulders and face, until only her eyes are uncovered.

I put my colcha aside, because I don't want to get it all dirty.

Besides, I don't want to fall asleep. I want for Mom and Dad to come home. I want to tell them about the secret door. I want to tell them about the creaking sounds. About the fallen bookcase.

They wouldn't believe you, my mind whispers. *They wouldn't. They'd just get mad again. Or worse, they'd laugh.*

"James?" Ava's sleepy voice calls out to me. "Should we call Mom?"

"No," I tell her as I slip down the slippery slope of sleep. . . . "It's daytime. We're safe up here."

It's daytime, and we are safe up here.

We are safe up here.

We are safe.

We are.

Safe.

I think.

CHAPTER 10

Between the uneasy feeling I get whenever I'm around him and the fact that he was standing right by our bikes when I got the second letter, Mr. Morris is our number one suspect for being the Keeper. That's why I've spent all of this Tuesday morning spying on him from up in this tree.

The huge oak is in our own backyard, so, technically, Ava and I aren't doing anything wrong. Though we both know if our parents come home early and find out we are snooping on our neighbors, they won't be too happy. But we only have three more days before the Blood Moon, so we don't have time to waste.

It doesn't take long to figure out where Mr. Morris lives. I watch him come out to pick up his mail as a woman pulls out of his garage in a nice red car around ten in the morning.

"That must be Betty, his daughter," Ava says, and she writes it down in her journal. I crawl from branch to branch, settling in different places and Ava draws in her journal, while we wait for him to go out on one of his "walks." Because he's actually the only suspect we have, we plan to follow him around. We think there's at least a small chance I'm not the only kid he's terrorizing. So, we hope to catch him in the act when he drops off one of those creepy letters to another kid in the neighborhood.

But the waiting drags on and on, and by twelve thirty, I am ready to jump down and go inside to make us something to eat. But then, Mr. Morris's daughter comes back. She pulls into their driveway, opens her trunk, and starts pulling out groceries.

"Come on! I have an idea!" I holler at Ava as I come down from the tree, grab her bag, and start running around to the front of the house.

"What are you doing?" Ava asks when she gets on her bike and follows me out of the driveway.

"I'm tired of wasting time," I tell her as I take to the street. "We need to get in there and talk to him. That's the only way we can figure out what he's all about."

"You mean, we ask him questions? Like on TV?" Ava cries when she sees me heading toward Mr. Morris's house.

"Noooo. That would be rude. We just . . . talk to him. Observe him. Try to figure out why he drags that red wagon all over town and why he takes the dogs for long walks at night. Things like that," I tell her, and I park my bike on the sidewalk, at the bottom of the Morrises' driveway.

"Got it," Ava says. "Good cop. Good cop."

I shake my head and sigh. "Just . . . follow my lead, okay?"

"I will!" Ava says, and she pushes down her kickstand and gets off her bike.

"Need some help?" I ask as we walk up to the red car.

Betty Morris lets a big bag go and turns to look at us, but she bumps her head on the trunk lid as she straightens up.

"Ouch," she cries out.

"Are you okay?" Ava asks, rushing over to check on her.

"Yes. Thank you. Silly me, I forgot that was there," Betty says, touching the trunk lid and then rubbing the back of her head gingerly.

"Sana sana colita de rana. Si no sanas hoy, sanarás mañana." Ava rattles off the familiar nursery rhyme.

Betty smiles at Ava. "I'll heal tomorrow, huh?"

"You understood the song?" Ava looks overjoyed. "We haven't met anyone else who speaks Spanish out here. But then again, we only just moved to Oregon a week ago."

"I just know a little Spanish," Betty admits. "What I remember from high school."

"Sana, Sana is the song of healing," Ava explains. "My mother sings it to us every time we get sick. She learned it from our Ita, my mother's mother. I'm Ava. And this is my brother, James."

"We just moved here from Texas," I say. "Can I take that inside for you?"

"Oh, yes. It's dog food," she says. "For the big guys! Dogs, I mean. We have two big dogs. I'm Betty, by the way."

"Glad to meet you," Ava says. "We met your dogs."

"And your father," I say, because that's why we're really here, to check him out. I pull at the huge bag of dog food and try to haul it out of the trunk, but it's heavy.

Ava grabs the other end of the dog food, and Betty takes the rest of her groceries out of the back seat of her car. Then she opens the garage door for me and Ava.

We're bringing the bag into the kitchen, when out of nowhere, two dark, enormous figures come running down the hall. The light coming in from the row of windows behind them makes it difficult to see what they look like, but we can hear their loud breathing. They sound like six-headed monsters! There is a clicking sound as the two beasts rush at us.

Ava screams as the beasts lunge. We both drop the bag of food, which splits open, scattering kibble across the floor. Then we turn around and run! But we don't get very far, because we bump right into Betty and her bags of groceries.

"Halt!" Betty calls and, suddenly, there is no more ruckus. "Sit."

Shocked, we turn around and gawk at the big, sad-eyed dogs. They are much bigger close-up and unleashed.

"Great Danes," Betty says. "They didn't mean to scare you. Trust me, they're cuddly teddy bears in big, overgrown bodies."

"What are their names?" Ava asks, looking at the huge dogs sitting perfectly still, side by side in front of us, looking more like puppies than fire-breathing dragons.

The Great Danes whine and lick their chops. They look

down at the bits of dog food scattered all over the tile floor like it's candy fallen out of a piñata.

"Oh, yes, introductions. Sorry, where are my manners?" Betty says, waving her hand in the air above the area where she hit her head. "Ava, James, these two magnificent creatures are Peanut Butter and his sister, Jelly. They're rescue dogs. We were fostering them last year, but they kind of grew on us, literally. Like they quadrupled in size. But we fell in love with them and now they're part of the family."

As if on cue, Peanut Butter and Jelly lower their heads and walk over to get to know us better. Their gangly legs move gracefully, and their nails click, click, click as they walk slowly across the floor.

Jelly sniffs my hands. Her monstrous snout whiffs me all the way up to my armpits, which makes me clam up, but only a little bit, because she's really gentle with her affection. Peanut Butter, however, goes crazy giving all kinds of doggy love to Ava, licking her hands and face as she cringes and giggles.

Betty grabs Peanut Butter and Jelly by their collars and pulls them off us. "Okay, that's enough love. Sit. Stay . . . No. No . . . leave the food alone," she warns, and the hounds whine, looking regretfully at all the spilled food they can't have.

"I've never seen dogs that big behave so well," I say as I reach down to pick up the torn bag of dog food off the floor.

Betty opens the pantry and pulls out a giant bin. She drags it across the floor and pries it open. With her help, Ava and I manage to pick up the bag of dog food and pour its contents into the bin. We're almost done when I hear the back door creak open.

"What happened here?" Mr. Morris asks as he walks into the kitchen, ignoring Betty when she introduces us.

"Oh, you know, the usual doggy shenanigans," Betty says. "Don't worry. I'll clean it up."

Mr. Morris reaches inside the pantry, pulls out a broom and dustpan, and hands the broom to his daughter. Betty starts sweeping the errant bits and pieces of dog food into a pile.

"It's our fault," I say, taking the broom from her.

Ava takes the dustpan from Mr. Morris. "We'll clean it up," she says.

Mr. Morris looks us up and down, but he doesn't say anything, and his face stays the same. He's like a stone. No reaction whatsoever. Then he turns away, takes a mug from its hook over the stove, and pours himself a cup of coffee.

Coffee in hand, Mr. Morris walks away and disappears down the hall.

Betty smiles. "He's not a people person," she says. "It comes from patrolling the forest alone all night for years. Even now that he's retired, he can't really get along with anyone. Other than me, of course."

"He used to patrol *this* forest?" I ask.

Betty nods and empties a grocery bag onto the counter. "Yup. Twenty-five years. He retired last December. But he still goes walking around all the time."

"Picking up trash," Ava says.

Betty's face changes. She frowns, but only for a moment. "Yes," she says, giving Ava a nervous little smile. "But just for a little while. He knows I don't like being here by myself."

"So, it is just you and your father, then?" Ava asks. "No mother. No brothers and sisters?"

I stop sweeping and glare at my sister. "Ava! That's none of our business." I know we're here to find out things about Mr. Morris, but I don't want Betty to think we're rude.

"That's okay," Betty says, waving at me. "There used to be four of us, before the divorce. I had a brother, Seth, but he . . . well, he's . . ."

I hear someone clearing their throat very loudly, and we all turn around to see Mr. Morris standing in the hall, holding the local newspaper neatly folded in his hand. His face, though, is more than stone-like.

It's downright grim.

Betty clamps her lips together. She turns away and starts unpacking another bag of groceries, putting an assortment of cans on the counter. She folds the empty paper sacks and quickly shoves them into a bin at the bottom of the pantry.

Mr. Morris puts the newspaper on the table and goes around us to get to the sink.

Ava raises her eyebrows at me and then stares down at the dustpan she's holding against the floor. I push at the pile of dog food.

127

"Thank you for doing that," Betty says as she stocks her pantry and refrigerator. Ava and I make quick work of cleaning up the spilled mess. When we are done, and I throw the last of the dirty kibble in the trash can, Peanut Butter and Jelly look very sad. They practically cry when they see me close the lid on the forsaken floor snacks.

"These two live for doggy bites." Betty takes the lid off a jar on the counter and throws Peanut Butter and Jelly a couple of biscuit-sized cookies that they catch, crunch, and pulverize before swallowing them down in seconds. "Mrs. Johnson bakes these for them. I think she's hoping to win them over."

"Stephanie's mom? They don't like her?" Ava asks.

Betty makes a face, like a half-smile half-cringe. Then she shrugs her shoulders. "I don't know why," she says. "I think she's lovely. But these two, well, they just can't seem to warm up to her."

"Everyone bakes around here," I say. "It's like a thing, isn't it?"

"Oh, yeah. It's the weather. It brings it out in people, I think." Betty pours herself a cup of coffee and takes a sip.

"Imagine that. Home-baked doggy treats." Mr. Morris stands at the counter and pulls out a doggy cookie from one of the jars on the counter and takes a bite out of it. "And they're good too. These guys love them."

Ava and I watch him eat the *cookie* and stare back at each other.

"Mrs. Johnson is very nice," I say, wondering why Mr. Morris would eat a dog treat with his coffee. Homemade or not, they're still meant for dogs.

"She's phenomenal. Best neighbor ever," Betty says. "She doesn't just bake treats. She does a lot of nice things for everyone in the neighborhood. Depending on the season, she puts together little baskets filled with teas, and fruits, and vegetables."

"Yes," Ava says. "She made one for my mother."

"But no one's better than Mrs. Benson," Betty continues. "She makes matching holiday wreaths for our doors and weaves personalized doormats. She even knits matching sweaters for PB&J every winter."

"Winter sweaters?" Ava squeals. "I bet they look cute."

I can't help it, I grin at the thought of seeing those giant dogs sitting around in their Christmas outfits. "Wow," I say. "That is nice."

"Mmmm. These new ones are good," Betty's father says as he pulls another dog treat out of the jar and offers it to us. "Would you like one?"

"No, thank you," I say, cringing a little at the thought of biting into it.

"How about you?" he asks, looking over at Ava.

"No!" Ava's eyes widen as she pulls back a little. "I don't . . . I can't . . . I'm sorry, but I only eat people food."

Betty quickly turns to look at the treat in her father's hand.

"Wait," she says. "No. Those aren't dog treats. Those are real peanut butter cookies. I baked them. To sell at the farmers' market. The doggy treats are in the other jar. Dad! Don't scare them like that!"

"Oh!" Ava and I breathe a sigh of relief.

"Okay," I say. "We thought you were eating dog food."

Mr. Morris turns to look at us. He presses his lips together and shakes his head. His big ears look enormous sticking out from his small bald head.

"Not my fault they scare easy," he tells his daughter as he walks past us and down the hallway again. "They need to toughen up if they're going to survive out here."

Betty apologizes to us as she sits at the table to drink her coffee. Because we agree to taste her home-baked treats, Betty puts together a plate of assorted cookies and pours out two glasses of milk.

We like her sugar cookies, and the Marionberry Drops are good too, but we all agree that the homemade Fancy Fig Squares are the best. They're better than anything we could get at the store. As we drink the last of our milk, Mr. Morris comes back into the room.

He stands by me, looks down, and nods at my scope hanging from its lanyard around my neck.

"That thing work all right?" he asks.

"Yes," I say.

"He likes to look at the stars with it," Ava says. "But we also go out to the woods to watch birds."

Betty frowns. Her hands start to shake, so she puts her coffee cup down. Suddenly, she looks worried. "Don't go very far. The woods are dangerous, and . . ."

Mr. Morris clears his throat loudly. Betty clams up. She

lowers her eyes and doesn't finish what she was saying. Then she looks up at her father and mumbles an apology.

"Well, since we're doling out advice," Mr. Morris says. "It's not safe to lie on your roof either. You could fall and break your neck."

The hairs on the back of my neck rise up, and I shiver. This is highly suspicious—Keeper-like knowledge—if you ask me. "How do you know about that?" I ask.

Mr. Morris turns his steel-gray eyes on me and gives me a piercing look.

"Oh, I see things. When I can't sleep, I go out and walk these two, and I see all kinds of strange goings-on." Mr. Morris uses his thumb to point back at Peanut Butter and Jelly, who are sprawled on the floor by the back door in the kitchen.

The dogs raise their heads, look at Mr. Morris, and whine.

"Oh, no, Dad," Betty whispers. "Now you've done it. You've said the W-word."

"Nonsense," Mr. Morris says. "They don't need a walk yet."

At the sound of the word, Peanut Butter and Jelly jump up and start barking. They bounce over to the spot in the kitchen where two very long, sturdy leashes hang from a hook on the wall.

"Dad, please," Betty says. "I can't walk them now. I have to start lunch."

"We'll walk them!" Ava pushes her chair back and stands up, knocking over her empty glass on the table. "Won't we, James?"

I turn to look at the two giants, waving their behinds,

practically bouncing off the tips of their toes, click, click, click-ing on the tile, as they frolic around, waiting for someone to walk them. "I . . . um . . ."

"Oh, come on," Ava says, and she pulls at my shirt until I stand up.

Mr. Morris frowns. "I'm not sure this is a good idea . . . The dogs . . . well, they're not always well behaved."

"What?" Betty gets up and takes the leashes off their hooks. "Don't listen to him. These two are very sweet," she says. "You just have to be firm with them, especially with Peanut Butter. He can be a handful if he thinks he can get away with it. But one good tug with an order to 'Sit' or 'Stay,' and they'll stop whatever they're doing."

Mr. Morris shakes his head. "Betty, I'm sure they have to go home. Children have their own chores to do."

"And our own dog to walk," I mumble.

"We can walk Baxter afterward," Ava says.

Mr. Morris shakes his head. "I'd rather you wouldn't. We don't want to be responsible . . . should something happen . . ."

"You're right, of course," Betty says, clutching the leashes in her hands and turning quickly to put them back.

Later, while we give Baxter his afternoon walk, we agree that Mr. Morris needs to stay on our list. The fact that he knows about my time on the roof is very unsettling. He gave us both a "creepy stalker" vibe.

As we walk around the neighborhood, Baxter is all over the

place. He doesn't obey my commands, mostly because he's having too much fun and isn't listening. Although, he's not too keen on taking the narrow dirt trail that leads to the secluded pond on the other side of the neighborhood. Ava and I have to practically drag him up there, with him whining the whole time. Once we get up there, however, Baxter is content to lie quietly beside Ava as she soaks her feet in the pond.

I take the opportunity to do some serious exploration of the forest through my trusty scope, getting right up to the edge of the tree line. Sitting on my haunches, I peer into the lens and see something moving in the darkest part of the woods, a giant black bird, frantically flapping its enormous wings.

Is it caught on something? I wonder.

I adjust the lens and find that there are other big black birds of prey around it, crows and buzzards and vultures, roosting on what looks like a small cemetery. As I move my scope from one end of the strange place to another, I count at least twenty-two tombstones.

The sight of those ancient-looking graves raises the hairs on the back of my neck, and I am reminded of the words *the last in a long line of Guardians of your house* from the Keeper's first letter.

Suddenly, I hear a small noise beside me, followed by a change in landscape, as something dark and blurry comes into view of my lens.

"¡Uy, Cucuy!" Ava screams.

Startled, I drop my scope and fall backward. And when I

look up, I see that Ava is using a plastic bag to hold up a desic-
cated black bird.

"Ava!" I cry. "What are you doing?"

"It's dead," she says.

"I can see that! Throw it away!" I get up, brushing the dirt off
my behind.

"No way," Ava says as she folds the plastic bag over the dead
bird. "I can dissect it. Figure out what happened to it."

"Do not put that thing in your bag. Mom would freak out if
she knew what you were up to right now," I say, taking it away
from her and dumping it in the nearest trash can. "Seriously,
why do you always have to pick up creepy, nasty things?"

Ava shrugs. "I have a scien-terrific mind," she says, grinning.
"It comes naturally."

"That's it. We're going home," I say, and I grab Baxter's leash
and start walking off with him. Baxter lopes around, prancing
ahead of me. "Come on. We shouldn't be out here."

"Awww! Do we have to?" Ava whines. She starts walking
behind me, but after a few yards I stop, turn around, and stand
completely silent. "Are you mad at me?" she asks.

"No," I tell her, ignoring her, because I can't get the picture
of those big black birds sitting around that cemetery out of my
mind. I think of the Keeper's letters again. The words *the last
in a long line of Guardians* are what's jumping out at me. I just
know there's something there. Something related to those old
tombstones.

I lift up my scope and look at that strange place in the woods again. It's so unbelievably spooky that I begin to question if I am not imagining things—if my mind isn't playing tricks on me. *Am I connecting two things that have nothing to do with each other?* I wonder.

"Hey," I say, stopping to wait for Ava. "Wanna go see something really creepy?"

Ava's left eye twitches nervously, and she reaches up and rubs it. "Where?"

"Out there." I point to the woods. "In the middle of the forest. I think it's a cemetery."

"A cemetery?" Ava's eyebrows rise high up on her forehead. "Really?"

"It might be . . . ," I whisper, trying to make sense of what I'm feeling—what my mind is still trying to work through. "It's very old."

"So? I don't see what that has to do with the Keeper," Ava says, and she waves me away.

"Well, the Keeper said he's *the last in a long line of Guardians of our house*," I say, walking slowly beside her. "Maybe, if we look at the tombstones, we'll find some names we can research. We might find out who used to live in our house."

Ava stops and thinks. "You might be onto something," she says. "Where is this *creepy* place?"

With Baxter smelling everything in our path, we walk into the dense part of the woods. Twigs snap under our feet and bushes claw at our clothes. I have to go in front of Ava so that I can push weeds and branches out of our way. However, as we start to walk around the cemetery, I hear someone moving in the woods.

"Wait!" Ava puts her hand on my arm, to make me stop. "Did you hear that?"

"Yeah," I say. "It's coming from over there."

Baxter sniffs, whines, and pulls back on his leash. "Maybe we should leave," Ava says as she holds on to Baxter. "Baxter doesn't think we should be here."

"Don't panic. It's probably just a deer or something," I tell her. Not convinced we should go, I pick up my scope and follow the movement of leaves on the trees.

That's when I see it, a person in a dark hoodie hidden deep in the woods, looking right at me from behind a set of binoculars. Startled, I drop my scope and pull Ava down, so we can duck behind a tombstone.

"What is it?" Ava asks. "What did you see?"

Before I can answer her, Baxter barks and takes off running across the cemetery.

"Baxter!"

"Baxter! No!" Ava and I yell after Baxter. But instead of listening to us, Baxter's going after the stranger in the woods, his leash flying behind him like a rebel flag.

"Come on!" I tell Ava, and we run after Baxter as fast as our legs will take us. Which is not very fast, because we have to weave around tombstones and fight our way through the thicket to the soft-beaten path that I didn't know was up there.

Up ahead, we see Baxter's caught up to the dark-clad figure. He's gotten ahold of the stranger's pants leg and is growling as he pulls on it with all his might. The frazzled stranger struggles, stumbles, and falls backward, crashing through the foliage as we reach them.

As we stand gasping on the edge of the narrow path, the stranger slips down a ravine, screaming. As the figure rolls over and over again, all the way down to the gulley below, I catch a glimpse of curly red tresses falling out and swirling around her hooded head.

"Whoa!" Ava says as the redheaded woman lands on the soft ground below with a thud. But she doesn't lie there very long. She scrambles up quickly and takes off running again.

Only one thought lingers in my mind as I watch her disappear into the woods. *I might not have seen her face, but I know exactly who that is.* "There's only one person in our neighborhood with curly red hair," I tell Ava.

Ava's eyes widen. "Ms. Phillips is the Keeper?!"

CHAPTER 11

Because we are more than a little shocked by our discovery, Ava and I rush right up to my room to talk in private when we get home.

"Wait," I tell Ava, because she's freaking out. She's walking back and forth across my room, talking too fast to be understood, going on and on about *cloaks* and *witches* and *secret paths* in the woods. I can't make any sense of it. "Slow down. Let's sit and calm down first. Okay?"

Ava nods and scoots herself onto my bed. Baxter gets up on the bed with her and she hugs him.

"What are we going to do?" Ava's eyes gleam with unshed tears. "We're just kids! We're no match for the Keeper!"

"First of all, we don't know for sure that Ms. Phillips is the Keeper," I say. "All we know is that she was watching us."

"And she ran away when we caught her!" Ava reminds me. "How much more guilty does she have to act?"

I shake my head. "Hmmm . . . maybe. But she could have

been scared of Baxter. He was trying to eat her pants."

"Okay, fine, but she was acting pretty creepy, don't you think?" Ava asks me. "We should call the police."

I remove the scope from around my neck and hang it over my desk chair. "I don't know about that," I tell her. "Maybe if we knew what she wants with us—with me. If we had some evidence of what she's trying to do, we could tell Mom and Dad."

"Do you really want to wait to find out what she wants?" Ava asks, holding tightly on to Baxter, who's looking back at me like he wants me to rescue him from Ava's anxious hug. "'Cause I don't. I'd rather have Mom and Dad call the sheriff right now. Tell him what we saw. Let him figure it all out. That's his job. To figure things out."

"They won't believe us. You know they won't." Frustrated, I scratch my head and plop myself down at my computer desk to think. "We need to spy on her, the way we did with Mr. Morris. We need to know what she does, where she goes, who she talks to . . ."

"If she's working with anyone," Ava chimes in.

"Yes. Everything," I say. "We need to know as much about her as she seems to know about us before that Blood Moon gets here."

Baxter whines and Ava lets him go. He sniffs around my bed and then curls up by Ava's feet. I think about how his barking was the only reason we know that Ms. Phillips was out there, and I'm grateful he was there to chase her away.

Ava pulls her legs up and hugs them in front of herself. She doesn't look as certain of this as I am. "I'm not sure that's going to work," she says. "I mean, she might just decide to lie low for a while."

"Then we'll have to sneak up to her house, peek in if we have to, see what she's up to," I tell her. "Because we need to find out what she was doing out there."

Ava sighs and pats Baxter's head gently, because he's falling asleep on my bed. "Well, wherever we go, we'll leave this guy behind," she whispers. "We can't let him ruin things again."

"Are you kidding?" I say. "Baxter's the best weapon we've got. He totally saved us today."

At dinner, Ava and I sit side by side at the table. It's not our usual place, but we need to face the front window so we can keep an eye on Ms. Phillips's house to see if she leaves again.

We do the same thing during family time, sitting on the love seat instead of the big sofa. Our parents don't mind. They're lying on the couch together. But Ava and I are too busy keeping an eye on Ms. Phillips's house to pay them any attention.

It's not until our father goes into the den to read his email and my mother gets busy in her office upstairs that we have an opportunity to sneak out of the house unnoticed.

"Here," Ava says, handing me my jacket. "It's raining out there."

I grab my scope and we head out the back door. Because it's drizzling, we walk quickly across the wet lawn and carefully clamber up the little incline behind our house.

We're not going very far, just to our oak tree in the backyard.

Even though it's slick and slippery, and I slide a couple of times, I am determined to climb it. It has the perfect view into Ms. Phillips's house.

"Be careful," Ava says. She's squatting on the ground, resting her back against the tree trunk with my mother's blue umbrella overhead because she's taking notes on what I find. Stealthily, I climb as high up as I can, wipe the rain off my face, and put my scope up to my right eye.

"The lights are on," I report. "In the living room, kitchen, and back porch."

Ava looks at my phone quickly and tucks it back in her pocket before she scribbles in her small notebook. "Seven thirty-five p.m., lights still on in LR, KT, and BP."

We wait for a long time, but nothing happens. The lights are on, but nobody's moving inside the house. At nine thirty, Ava starts complaining.

"Maybe we should just go inside," she whines. "It's late, and I'm tired. She's obviously not going back out tonight. It's raining too much."

If you don't act before the sun covers the moon's face, you put everyone and everything in danger. The Keeper's words creep into my mind, haunting me.

"We can't afford to sleep," I tell Ava. "The Blood Moon is on Friday. We have to figure this out sooner rather than later."

"Stupid Blood Moon," Ava mumbles. "It's not even a scientific term. It's a total lunar eclipse. That's what it's really called."

"Oh, oh—we have movement!"

"Movement? Really?" Ava asks. "Where? Which room?"

I twist the lens on my scope, so I can get a clearer picture. "She's in the kitchen," I say.

Ava looks at the time on my phone and scribbles in her notebook. "What's she doing?"

"She's on the phone," I tell her. "Come on, let's go!"

"Go? What do you mean, go?" Ava asks as I drop my scope.

"Hurry. We have to find out who she's talking to." I jump down, land on the soggy ground beside her, and help her up.

Ava and I run across the street, past the grassy knoll, as fast as we can until we are hiding in the bushes just outside Ms. Phillips's kitchen window. We watch Ms. Phillips shake her head and wave her arm around while she talks.

"No. No. No," she keeps saying. "I went all the way out there, and they weren't doing anything wrong!"

"Who do you think she's talking to?" Ava asks.

"Shhh . . ." I put my finger up to my lips and scoot closer to the window.

"Of course they followed me!" Ms. Phillips hisses at whoever is on the phone with her. "Their mutt tried to kill me!"

Mutt? Offended, Ava mouths the word at me.

Agitated, Ms. Phillips gets louder. "I have to go. My hip still hurts and now I have a headache."

And with that, Ms. Phillips ends the call and puts the phone down on the counter beside her. She looks around the kitchen and then picks up her phone and leaves the room, turning out the lights behind her.

Because we can't see where Ms. Phillips went in the house, Ava and I creep away and rush back to our house. Up in the tree again, I move forward, crawl onto the nearest branch, inching myself over it a bit at a time, observing Ms. Phillips as she sits watching TV in her living room.

"I wish I knew who she was talking to!" I say, creeping over to the next drenched branch. "Who asked her to follow us out there."

"I don't know," Ava says. "But it certainly sounded suspicious."

"Oh, now she's shutting herself in."

"Shutting herself in?" Ava sounds confused. "What do you mean?"

"Well, she's checking all the windows and pulling down the blinds. So, that's it for now," I tell her, shifting from one branch to another, trying to find the best way to get back down. "I can't see inside the house anymore."

At that very moment, thunder roars in the distance, lightning crawls across the sky, blinding me, and I stop and freeze. I close my eyes against the strong wind that sweeps in under the tree and listen as a loud, hissing, metallic sound cuts through the silence.

Zzzzzzzzzzzzzzzooooooommmmmm!

I hear a snap, and suddenly, the branch breaks and falls out from under me.

I jump.

Hurl myself forward. Tuck and roll. And end up flat on my back on the ground.

"James!" Ava's scream pierces the darkness, shatters the silence.

"I'm all right! I'm all right!" I say, touching my head, feeling the sore spot on my left temple. It's wet in a different way than rain is wet. Blood, I think. But I don't tell Ava because I don't want to scare her.

"You're bleeding!" Ava cries as she shines the phone on my face. "Oh, my God, James! You broke your head!"

The lights on our back porch come on, and I can hear footsteps running toward us.

"James? Ava?" my father calls.

"Jaimito! Are you all right, m'ijo?" my mother asks as she kneels down on the soggy ground beside me. "What happened?"

"I'm fine. I'm fine. I just fell. From the tree," I say, sitting up as my mother puts her hands on my cheeks and inspects my face.

"We need to clean that scrape right away," my mother says. "Can you move? Do you need my help?"

"The tree?" my father asks. "This late at night? What were you all doing up there?"

"Spying . . ." Ava slaps her hand over her mouth, and all we see is two wide eyes staring back at us.

"We were playing Mission Impossible," I explain. "Spies in Berlin. But the branch snapped under me."

"I don't think it snapped," Ava says, shining my phone's flashlight on the fallen branch beside her. "That wasn't a break. That's a clean cut."

My father leans over and touches the smooth edge of the broken branch. "That's strange," he says. "It's like someone took a saw to it. See that?"

"That doesn't make sense," my mother says. "If it was sawed all the way through . . . then how did it stay up there?"

"I heard a weird noise. Just before . . . ," I start, but then I stop, because I'm not sure what I heard or if it's even related to the accident.

My father shakes his head.

"Come on, let's get out of this rain," he says. And we all follow him into the house.

My father sits next to me on the couch while Ava runs to get the first aid kit for the second day in a row so that my mother can clean the wound on my forehead.

"Climbing over broken branches!" she says. "Maybe you should be more careful. I'm worried about you."

"That branch wasn't broken when I climbed up there," I remind her. "I felt it . . . I heard it when it happened . . . It was like it was being sawed off right from under me."

"You mean like . . . something *supernatural*? Like magic?" Ava asks. Thunder roars in the distance and we all stare at her.

I shake my head. "Nope. I don't believe in magic."

"I'm sure there's a reasonable explanation for it," my father says, breaking the silence. "Facts are stranger than fiction. I'll do some research tomorrow."

"This wasn't a coincidence," my sister says, looking over at me. "Someone made this happen."

"Who would do something like that?" my mother asks. "Who could make a sawed tree branch stay up like that?"

"The question isn't *who*," I tell them, looking into the darkness outside the living room window, beyond the knoll in front of our house. "The question is *why*."

"Well, I'm just glad you didn't break anything," my mother says. "Nothing feels broken, right?"

"No, nothing's broken," I say, and to prove it I move my arms and lift my knees. "See? I'm fine."

"Well, you were lucky." My mother reaches up and pulls a tiny twig out of my hair and hands it to me.

"Listen," my father starts. "Climbing that soaked tree was really dangerous. Do me a favor. From now on, play in your room or at least stay on the ground when it's raining."

When we are alone in the living room, playing a video game on the big screen, Ava leans over and whispers, "Do you think this is worth it? I mean, as much as I want Ms. Phillips arrested, I think something more dangerous is happening here."

"What are you trying to say?" I ask.

Ava leans in so that only I can hear her. "I think we should quit while you're still in one piece," she whispers.

I look back to the kitchen, to make sure our parents can't hear us.

"Are you saying . . . that you want to stop trying to figure this out?"

Ava raises the volume on the controller, so that the noise from the video game disguises our conversation. "I'm saying . . . two letters, two accidents. That's not a coincidence, James. That's like a sign. I think it's time we slow down."

"You wanna slow down? Three days before the Blood Moon?" I ask, making my avatar go into a deep jungle to look for food and shelter. "Like, forget we ever got the letters? Forget that someone out there is stalking our family?"

"Well, when you put it that way." Ava sighs, leans back, and stares at her frozen avatar on the screen as if she doesn't know how to control it.

"I think these accidents prove one important thing—Ms. Phillips is the Keeper. And she means business," I say. "If we don't find evidence of it to—put her away for good—we could all . . ."

On the screen, Ava and I die and the game ends. I hit the restart button on the controller and the video game begins again. Ava's avatar leads the way through the jungle, and I follow her quietly.

"Well?" I ask her as I shoot up an arsenal in a small hidden compound.

"Okay, fine!" Ava says, raising her voice as she settles back on the couch with a huff. "Are you happy? I'm in again!"

"Are you two fighting?" my mother asks, calling out to us from the kitchen, where she is prepping tomorrow's meals.

Ava lifts her head and yells back, over the couch, "No! We're not!"

"We're a team, Mom!" I yell after her. "We're better than that."

CHAPTER 12

When I wake up, Ava is sitting at my desk with Baxter by her side.

"Well, so much for Ms. Phillips," she says, petting Baxter's head.

I push the hair out of my face and look for my phone because we went to bed so late last night that I can't remember if I plugged it in. "What are you talking about?" I ask, leaning over and looking under the bed.

Ava gets up and comes over to the side of my bed.

"She's gone," she says, waving my phone in front of my face. "She packed up and left."

"Thanks." I take the phone from her. *Yup. It's dead. I forgot to plug it in.* "Left?" I ask. "What do you mean, she left?"

"Yeah. She just picked up her tiliches and disappeared. Poof." Ava snaps her fingers. "Just like that."

I push the covers off and sit on the edge of the bed, wondering what this all means. "You saw her?"

"No, of course not. She left in the middle of the night,"

Ava says. "Mrs. Coleman brought over some scones early this morning. She told Mom she put extras in there because she didn't know Ms. Phillips was already gone until she went over there. She said Ms. Phillips probably went down to California, to visit her sister for a few weeks. She does that every year about this time."

"Well, that's convenient, isn't it?" I say.

"What do you mean?" Ava asks, sitting at the foot of the bed.

I take the cord from my nightstand and plug in my phone. "Well, think about it," I tell her. "We caught her stalking us and now she's suddenly gone. Does she think we're that dumb or something?"

Ava looks out the window. "You think she's still out there?"

"Do I think she's hiding?" I ask. "Yeah. Absolutely. You heard how upset she was . . . She only *wants* us to believe she's gone."

Ava's eyes glimmer as she thinks about what I've said. "That makes sense," she says. "But I don't think she's the one we have to worry about. Whoever she was talking to on the phone last night had a lot to say about the situation."

Suddenly, another possibility enters my mind. And I wonder if I'm reading too much into this. "Wait a minute . . . ," I whisper as I try to sort through the wild thoughts that are rushing into my mind like an avalanche.

"What if she didn't leave?" I start. "What if someone made her . . . disappear."

My sister's eyes widen. "Someone who got upset with her because she didn't want to work with them anymore!" Ava lets

149

loose a shiver as she finishes my thought. "Oooooh . . . I didn't even think about that."

"We can't dismiss anything or anyone," I say, forcing myself to fight through the fear that is starting to unfurl and writhe in the pit of my stomach. The Keeper's words, *Like this community, your house is very special. Go ahead, explore it, try to uncover its many secrets,* are tumbling around in my mind. "Everyone in this place is a suspect. Even Mrs. Coleman, for delivering the news. She could be working with Ms. Phillips, or she could be working with the real Keeper."

"Or worse," Ava whispers. "*She* could be the Keeper."

"You know what that means, don't you?" I ask. "With the Blood Moon almost here and our main suspect gone, we don't have time to waste. We have to rev up this investigation."

Ava nods. "We need to go back to the cemetery," she says. "Research every name on those tombstones. Find out who these people are, once and for all!"

When we have a plan, I get dressed and run downstairs in a rush. The rain from the night before has been reduced to nothing more than a mild misting, so that, after breakfast, Ava and I set out to investigate the cemetery beyond the pond.

Though we don't exactly know what the Keeper means when he says we're putting *everyone and everything in danger,* we both agree with our stalker. It's *time to make something happen.*

There are no walking trails that we know of to the cemetery, so Ava and I make our way to the pond, hoping we'll be able to see some sort of path that will lead us in the right direction. We're looking through my scope for a better way through the forest when Jack, Ronnie, Stephanie, Daniel, Dave, Paul, Laurie, Sam, and Beth walk up to us.

"Hey!" Jack says, when he gets within earshot. "So, this is where you've been hiding!"

Jack and the team are all dressed warmly because the rains have turned the days cool. "What's up?" I ask him.

"Nothing. Just going down to Whitebark, to get a little practice in," he says. "Are you two coming out today? We missed you yesterday."

"If the rain gets going again, like it did yesterday, we might not," Ava says.

Stephanie and her twin brothers, Daniel and Dave, look at each other and snicker.

"What's so funny?" I ask.

"Nothing," Stephanie says, fighting to keep the grin off her face. "It's just that people who aren't from here are so afraid of the rain. It's just a little funny, that's all."

Ava's face darkens. I can see she's embarrassed. "There's nothing funny about the rains up here," my sister says. "You've got flooding and mudslides, and all kinds of nasty environmental things happening because of it. I know. I looked it up."

Stephanie's eyebrows knit over her forehead, and she thinks for a moment. "I've never heard of any flooding or mudslides in our neighborhood," she says, looking out at the forest beyond the pond. "My mother says that can't happen here. Not in our town."

"Seriously?" Ava asks. "You can't predict that. Natural disasters happen. Everywhere. To everyone."

Stephanie laughs again, and Daniel and Dave start laughing too, but then she puts her hand up to her lips to make herself stop.

"You're not really scared, are you?" she asks. "We've never had anything crazy happen to us. Not even the forest fires affect us. Not out here."

"Never say never," Ava mumbles under her breath.

"My mother says we're blessed," Dave says. "Nothing like that will ever touch us!"

"Then your mother's sonsa!" Ava says.

"Ava!" I call out. "That's not nice."

"What?" Ava asks. "She started it!"

"I'm sorry," I say, looking up at Jack and Ronnie, who've stayed out of the dumb argument between Ava and Stephanie. "I'm not sure we can make it today. Maybe in a couple of days."

Jack shakes his head. "Nope. Not during the Blood Moon."

The Blood Moon!

Thunder rolls in the distance, and I look behind me, where a whip of white light lashes across the gray-blue sky.

"The Blood Moon?" Ava questions. "What about the Blood Moon?"

"It's nothing," Ronnie says. "Just an old wives' tale."

"It's kinda dumb, but our parents still don't want us playing outside," Jack says.

The others remain silent, but Beth rolls her eyes and crosses her arms in front of her. "So, we're really not gonna play because of the Blood Moon?" she asks. "Guys! It's just a bunch of nonsense. My mother says it's a regular day and we should do regular things. Besides, she's got a special treat planned for us on that day. My big sister's visiting from out of town, so she's trying to perfect her cookie recipes!"

"Sorry," Ronnie says. "No can do."

Beth shrugs and starts to turn away.

"Well, we're still practicing today," Jack says, looking back at me. "If you wanna join us later."

Ava narrows her eyes and looks at Stephanie. "*My mother* might not let us. James had an accident, and . . ."

"An accident?" Jack looks startled. His eyebrows are crinkled together on his forehead and he's looking at me like he's worried. "What kind of accident? You didn't hurt your batting arm, did you? I mean, you can still make the ball fly, right?"

"Oh, no," Ava says, waving a hand in the air. "His arm is fine. It's not that. We're actually—"

"Let's play it by ear," I say, interrupting Ava. I'm not sure why but I get the feeling she's about to give too much away. I don't want Jack and the others to think we're doing anything else out here other than bird watching. "I'll see what my parents say. They might have something planned for us. They like to do that kind of thing, make family rituals out of everything."

"Rituals?" Stephanie makes an ugly face, which makes me think I'm not sure I like her. "What kind of rituals?"

"Oh, you know, the usual," I say. "Things to do together."

"Family things," Ava explains. "To keep us connected. Family Movie Night, Family Game Night, Family . . ."

"Yeah, well, it's . . . my father's idea," I admit. "He likes us all to hang out in the evenings."

"I get it," Beth says. "Well, have a good Family 'Whatever' Night, if you don't make it out."

Jack nods. "You know where we'll be if you change your mind," he says, and he turns and walks away. All the other kids follow him.

"Don't you think it's weird?" Ava asks when the kids are far enough down Pine Circle that they can't hear us. "How they acted about this place? Like nothing wrong could ever happen here. Boy, are they living in a dreamworld or what?"

"It's not weird," I say as I turn away from Jack and the kids and start walking along the pond, so that we can get to the other side. "Kids tend to believe everything their parents say. We do, don't we? Believe Mom and Dad, I mean."

"Sure," Ava says, turning to look back at the surface of the pond. "But our parents don't keep us from playing outside because of the Blood Moon! And don't you think that's creepy?"

"How they're not going to play on the same day that the Keeper said was our last day to figure this out?" I ask.

"Wait a minute. . . . Do you think . . . ," Ava starts. "Could this be a great big prank? I mean, do you think Jack and them could be . . . ?"

"No," I tell her.

"No?" Ava stares me down. "Why not?"

"Because something about Ms. Phillips's disappearance feels like a lot more than a prank," I tell her as I stop and stare at the tree line before us. The mist is starting to thicken to a drizzle, and I zip up my rain jacket. Above the tree line, I see birds again, big black birds, circling around and around, and a shiver runs up my spine. "I really think the Keeper's out there, watching our every move."

"Do you think it's safe? Going into the woods like this?" Ava asks as she looks up at the dark flock of birds soaring overhead. "Without letting anyone know where we're going?"

"No," I say. "But how else are we supposed to figure this out? Come on, I think we can go in through here."

Together, Ava and I try our best to find a good place to enter the woods, a place where the trees are not as dense. Finally, after about a quarter of an hour, we decide to take the plunge.

I push back branches with my forearms, and though the pine trees are not hard to move, there are all kinds of thick bushes growing around them. Things with bristles and thorns and spikes tear at our clothes and scratch our faces. But we keep going, until we finally get there.

"Well, that was an epic fail," Ava says when we can't read half the names on those crumbling old tombstones.

"No it's not. You got a decent list there," I tell Ava as we round the bend and head back up Pine Circle, toward our house. "It's a good start. We can look up family trees. Go to genealogy sites.

Don't worry. We'll figure this out."

"So, are we back to thinking it could be Mr. Morris?" Ava asks, looking up at me through her rain-drenched eyelashes.

"Well, with Ms. Phillips gone, he's the only suspect we can investigate right now. You don't want to dismiss him, do you?" I ask her.

Ava shakes her head. "No. He's still my number two suspect, for sure."

When we get back to the house, Ava and I hurry up the stairs. We split up the jobs, to make this quicker. And while I look up the names on the tombstones on my phone, Ava looks into ancient stories about the Blood Moon on my computer. She wants to see what people in Oregon believe about it. She's not having much luck, though.

"It's just a bunch of superstitious stuff," she moans. "If you understand, you can tell none of this is real. Even the scientists who say the moon moves the tides agree it can't cause bad things to happen. Not really. There's no evidence the Blood Moon affects people or nature."

"But what it does prove," I say, "is that the Keeper believes those things. Which means they must be superstitious."

"Don't you think it's strange?" Ava says, swiveling around in my desk chair. "How Stephanie kept insisting nothing bad ever happens here? Like they're special or something."

"Look it up," I tell her, distracted, because Mike sent me a text message.

MIKE: hey, how's practice going?
making some progress?
BETO: mike and i are about to go in
for preseason at school,
like we planned
MIKE: wish you were here
it would be triple threat
all over again
ME: for sure

As I type a reply, I think about all the plans Mike, Beto, and I made together. Sixth grade was going to be our breakout year. We were going to try out for everything. Work on being more athletic. Figure out what else we're good at, other than baseball. This move to Oregon changed everything. I'm waiting for Mike or Beto to respond to my last text when another text comes through. From a number I don't recognize.

Unknown Number: Hey, James. Can we talk?

Unknown number. Capital letters. Punctuation. My stomach knots up as Keeper-vibes crawl up from my phone, seep into my fingertips, and rush up the length of my arms, making me shiver.

Ava taps away at my keyboard. I stare at the phone and wonder what I should do.

ME: who is this?

The message goes through. I watch it sit there, all by itself on the right side of the screen, and then another text comes in.

BETO: are you going to try out for a team there?
with your new bffs?
ME: new bffs?
what's wrong with
making new friends?
MIKE: dude, don't be rude
Don't listen to him james
you gotta live your life

I stare at the exchange. Is Beto upset? Does he think I've replaced him and Mike with other kids out here? I mean, I haven't. Mike and Beto are my best friends in the whole wide world. They're . . .

Unknown Number: Sorry, my mom was calling me.
This is Jack, BTW.

As I read the words again, I sigh with relief. So weird. I didn't know I was holding my breath.

ME: jack? how did you get my number.
JACK: Your sister gave it to us.

Anyway, we missed you today.

I hope Stephanie didn't offend you.

"You gave my number to Jack?" I ask Ava.

She turns back to look at me sitting on the edge of my bed having two very awkward conversations at the same time.

"Oh, yeah," Ava says, turning back to the computer screen. "I made a list of all the team members and passed it out. I put yours over here, next to the computer. You didn't see it?"

I look at the small piece of folded notebook paper to the right of the computer. "No," I say, looking down at my phone again. "I haven't been at my computer the last few days."

Ava ignores me again as she taps and reads and taps and reads.

JACK: She didn't upset you, did she?

She can be kind of mean sometimes.

But I can talk to her if you want.

ME. nah, I'm all right

JACK: Good. Sorry we can't play on Friday.

Can't be helped.

Parents, you know.

ME: I know.

JACK: But I hope you can join our team

We need you in the league.

ME: Thanks.

I want to tell him I have other things to think about, things that he couldn't understand, but I don't feel comfortable talking to him. If this was happening back home, I would have told Beto and Mike right away. But they're over two thousand miles away from here. They couldn't do anything to help if they tried.

BETO: that's okay. you can try out if you want
but you're not going to get far without us
ME: what about you?
you got no chance without me
BETO: without cooties?
ME: ouch!
BETO: kidding!
MIKE: miss you hermano
ME: me too
gn
MIKE: gn
BETO: hasta luego

I'm sitting there, thinking how strange it is to be torn between two teams . . . two sets of friends . . . two worlds . . . wondering if I'm going to survive and someday figure out where I belong when Ava jerks in her chair.

"James," Ava says in a hushed, troubled whisper.

"What?" I ask, putting my phone aside.

"There's something going on in this place," she says, her eyes wide. "Stephanie was right. Nothing bad ever happens in this neighborhood!"

I get up to look at the screen. "What are you talking about?"

"It's true," Ava whispers. "Well, look at all these articles. It's like this place *is* blessed. I found a bunch of stories about it in the Portland paper. Look at this one. It says the wildfires hit Oregon hard the last few years. They were everywhere. Except here. They haven't touched one tree in this forest. And this other article says the mudslides always go around this community. Even the economic crisis that affected the whole country last year didn't affect Brentville. The town's budget stayed strong the whole time. Don't you think that's weird?"

"Very weird," I say as I take the mouse and click on the different tabs at the top of the screen to scan the articles.

"It's like they're . . . protected," Ava says.

I know where she's headed with this, but I refuse to believe it.

Magic is absolutely *not* real.

CHAPTER 13

After dinner, I decide to go up to my room instead of watching TV with my family. As I lie in bed, I can't stop thinking about all those articles Ava found. Though I didn't get anything on the names from the list, just a bunch of old obituaries, I'm wondering what's going on in this town. There has to be an explanation for why Brentville is so safe. The idea that nothing bad ever happens here also seems so at odds with getting scary letters from some mysterious stranger.

All I want to do is figure out who is sending those creepy letters and why, but nothing makes sense. Though it's clear Ms. Phillips is not the Keeper, I don't know if Mr. Morris is either. Other than his comments about me lying on the roof, I don't know if he's superstitious enough. And Mrs. Benson; her husband, Henry; Mrs. Martin; and Mr. Brent are too nice. They would never do anything like this.

Jack's father, Mr. Harvey, seems nice too. He made all that

food for us, and he didn't even complain about having to start all over again when I messed things up. Remembering about all the trouble I caused for everyone that day makes me cringe. But thinking about the fact that any one of those people at the barbecue could be the Keeper freaks me out, and I jump off the bed and go to the window.

I peer out into the yard. But only for a moment, before I pull the curtains shut, making sure there is absolutely no gap through which anyone can catch a glimpse of me. My legs shaking, I crawl back into bed and quickly scroll through my video collection of my Ita's "Consejos From the Other Side" until I find what I'm looking for.

In the video, my Ita's wearing a regal purple dress with tiny silver stars floating along the edge of her neckline. Her big chunky earrings match the silver stars perfectly. They twinkle and shine as she laughs at something I said before I started recording. But when she looks into the camera, her eyes say *I love you* in a way that makes me feel all warm inside. And, suddenly, I am safe and secure again.

"Remember, you must never be afraid," she whispers. *"The ancestors are always with you, watching over you, guiding you when you go astray. Our antepasados, our parents, grandparents, great-grandparents, and all their parents before them, are our celestial guardians. Rest easy, Jaimito. You have divine protection."*

Even though she's talking about magic, the way she explains

it, magic is a good thing. It comes from believing that your family will always be there for you, even when they're gone, like guardian angels.

As the last in a long line of Guardians of your house . . . The words from the Keeper's letters come into my mind again, and I shudder. Then I pull my colcha over my head and play Ita's video over and over again, because it makes me feel better to know she's watching out for me, for us.

"What are you doing?" My father pulls back the covers. I jump and drop the phone. It lands on the bed beside me. I pick it up and shut it off quickly.

"Nothing," I say. "I was just . . . watching videos of Ita."

"Aww. You missing your guelita?" my father asks as he straightens the cover over me, gives it a good tug, and pushes the edges under the mattress so that I am officially tucked in.

"Always," I say, and I put my phone down on top of my chest. "She told the best stories. And gave the best consejos."

My father smiles, that thin little smile that tells me he gets it. "Well, I certainly understand that," he says. "She was pretty special."

"Is," I say. "I still have her. Right here."

"Well, it's time for bed," he says. "Can you put the phone away, for now?"

"Bed?" I ask. "It's not even eleven."

"Eleven is late," my father says. "Some of us have to work in the morning."

"But my phone won't keep you up," I say. "That's what headphones are for."

My father scratches his head. He takes a deep breath and lets it out, exasperated.

"It's not about the noise," he finally says. "You just can't stay up all night, James. It's not healthy."

"But it's summertime," I whine.

My father's wry smile shows he's just about had it with me, but I press on anyway. "School doesn't start again for three more weeks."

"That's precisely why you need to stop staying up all night," he says. "You've got to start synchronizing your body. Think of this as baby steps. Eleven o'clock this week. Ten next week. Nine the next week. And then, you're all set. You'll get nine hours of rest every night and jump out of bed bright and early by the time school comes around. Okay?"

"Augh!" I let the noise escape my lips and roll my eyes.

My father crosses his arms in front of himself and laughs.

"What?" he asks. "Am I making too much sense? It's true, isn't it? I'm making sense."

"Adult sense. Not kid sense," I mumble as I lean over and feel under my bed for the cord to charge my phone.

My father reaches down and hands me the neon-blue cord. I plug in my phone and set it facedown on my nightstand.

"We need to get you one of those charging pads," my father says as he leans over and kisses my forehead.

"Nah," I say. "I'd just knock the phone off in the middle of the night."

"You're not having pesadillas, are you?" my father asks.

"No," I say. "I haven't had nightmares for a long time."

My father stands there for a moment longer before he turns to leave. At the door, he stops. "Try to stay off your phone, son. And don't go out to lie on the roof anymore. It's dangerous," he says. When I look at him, shocked, my father nods. "Yeah. I know about that! Good night. Love you, boy."

"I love you too," I whisper as my father closes the door behind him.

I lie in bed for at least an hour, tossing and turning. And because I can't go to sleep, I get up and turn on my computer. Now that I don't have anything to distract me, I can concentrate on researching the names on the tombstones.

Going through newspapers doesn't help. But after a few hours I finally find a good ancestry website that lets me look at all kinds of records with a fourteen-day free membership without a credit card. What I find when I plug in all the information I have from each tombstone gives me the shivers. I sit at my desk for a while, just staring at my notes. So many thoughts come in and out of my mind. *Should I wait till morning to show Ava? Is it too scary? Will it freak her out as much as it does me?*

Because I've been up for a long time, my stomach starts to rumble. I know I won't be able to sleep if I don't eat something. So, I fold up my notes, shove them into my pajama pocket with my phone, and go downstairs to make myself a midnight snack.

Everything in the house is dark and silent. I don't want to wake anyone, so I creep past Ava's room and tiptoe across the carpeted floors even though I'm in my socks. And when I reach the stairs, I take one step at a time, because my parents' bedroom is close by.

The first step creaks, the second one moans, but the third and fourth one squeak and squawk so loud, I'm sure I'm going to get caught. My father doesn't like it when we mess up the kitchen after he's cleaned it up for the night. But I can't help it. I'm hungry. And only a big, juicy, roast beef sandwich with queso fresco is going to change that.

I don't turn on the kitchen's overhead light. Instead, I flip the switch on the hood over the range. It's bright enough for me to see what I'm doing as I rummage around in the refrigerator for everything I need. Roast beef, queso fresco, lettuce, tomato, no onions—thank you very much—and, ah yes, mayonnaise. Can't make a good sandwich without mayonnaise.

I place a couple of slices of sourdough bread on my plate and start putting together my sandwich. And when I'm done, I step back and take a good look at it. Perfection. But wait, I need a pickle. I look in the refrigerator, and when I can't find any I open the walk-in pantry and spot a new jar of dill pickles on the top corner shelf. I stand on my tippy-toes and reach for it. And just as I put my fingertips on it, I hear a noise.

Creeeeaaaaaak . . . . . .

I freeze.

Is that a door?

"Ava?" I call out quietly. "Is that you?"

Creeeeaaaaaak . . . .

"Stop it," I tell her. "I know it's you. You can't scare me!"

Creeeak. Creeeak. Creeeak.

I slip the jar off the shelf and wait in the dark pantry, holding the pickles close to my chest. I don't want to admit it, but I am a little bit spooked. Not scared, just spooked. I listen, but all I can hear is the rhythmic sound of my own heartbeat thundering violently against my eardrums.

Creeeak. Creeeak. Creeeak.

I lean over and try to look into the kitchen. But all I see is the sink with its neatly folded dishrag hanging from its metal hook. *Wait . . . is that a shadow creeping over the floor?*

"I see you," I tell her quietly. "You better leave my sandwich alone!"

Suddenly, the shadow moves—rushes toward me.

I jump, and almost drop the jar of pickles.

"Baxter!" I say in a harsh whisper, when I see Baxter standing in front of the pantry door in the dimly lit kitchen. "What are you doing down here? Where's Ava, huh?"

I walk over to the end of the counter and flip the light switch. Immediately, the kitchen is illuminated. Light bathes the room, engulfs me, blinds me. And, when my eyes adjust, I take a good look around. But everything's the same. And my sandwich is intact.

"Good boy," I tell Baxter softly as he lifts his head and sniffs at the counter.

"James?" Ava walks into the kitchen rubbing her eyes. "What's going on? What are you doing down here?"

"I was researching those names on the list, and I got hungry. So, I came down to make myself a sandwich," I say in a hushed whisper. "I thought I was alone, until Baxter came down here. He scared me. I almost dropped the pickles."

"Well? Did you find anything?" Ava asks quietly, and she sits on the nearest stool. "About the people on the list?"

I take a deep breath and put the pickles on the counter, next to my sandwich, so that I can pull my notes out of my pajama pants. "Yes," I whisper, holding the folded paper tightly between my fingertips. "Are you sure you're ready to read this? I'm not trying to scare you, but it's pretty creepy stuff."

Ava stares me down. "James!" she says softly. "Don't drag this out." And she yanks the paper out of my hand.

"They were kids, Ava," I hiss as she unfolds the paper and starts reading. "Those four, right there. This one was ten. These two were eleven. And this one was only nine. Nine, Ava."

"Kids . . ." Ava lets the word sink in. "Okay. Children died and were buried. What's creepy about that? I mean, it's tragic, but, you know, it happens. More back then than now, I'm sure."

"Yeah, but did you see the dates?" I ask her. "They all died exactly twenty-five years apart, give or take a few days."

"Now that's creepy," Ava whispers as she studies my notes. I watch her little mouth twist as she thinks about what she's reading. "Hold on. Can I see your phone?"

"What for?" I ask her, pulling my phone out of my pocket and handing it to her. "Trust me. There's nothing else out there about them. I know. I spent hours poking around."

Ava does a quick search.

"I knew it," she whispers as she flips the phone up and shows me the screen. "He passed away during a Hunter's Moon."

I stare at the lunar calendar displayed on my phone. "What?"

Ava searches the names of the other two children on my list. "And she passed during a Super Blood Moon."

To our horror, we discover that all four children died during some kind of total lunar eclipse!

"James . . . what are we going to do?" Ava wraps her arms around my waist and hugs me so tight, I can't catch my breath. My heart is pumping wildly inside my chest as I hug my sister back, because I don't know what else to do.

That's when it happens. The window flies open, and a strong gust of wind rushes into the room, blowing the frilly yellow curtains up into the air.

Ava and I stare, both surprised and horrified, as a familiar piece of paper comes flying in through the window. The curtains flutter as the paper rolls and rolls, doing all kinds of flips, as it flies over us and then turns around, like a boomerang, and starts to glide gently over us, until it lands, right side up, against the jar of mayonnaise.

Ava and I stare at the envelope. We rush to the window to

see who tossed in the envelope, but the night is dark and still. There's nobody out there.

"I know you don't believe in magic," Ava whispers. "But that's what that was . . . wasn't it? I mean, I didn't imagine it. Did I?"

My eyes burn, and I fight back the tears and the fear. The realization that magic is very much what's behind the Keeper's actions makes my whole body shake. "No. That just happened."

Beside me, Ava is silent. The hall, the dinner table, the window, everything is silent. Everything except the envelope, with its long, elegant letters staring back at me.

Taunting me.

—James Anthony McNichols—

I walk toward it.

"James!" Ava whispers, and she leaves the window to get closer to me.

"I know," I tell her softly as I put my arm around her shoulders, because she is shaking, and she looks like she's about to cry too.

"Are you going to open it?" she asks.

"Do I have a choice?" I ask as I take a deep breath. I pick up the envelope, hold it for a moment, and then release it when my lungs start to hurt.

I look around again. Without moving my head, I look at the window in front of us. *Is the Keeper watching us now, from somewhere in the darkness?* I wonder. *Does he know how scared we are?*

Just read it! my mind screams.

With my sister beside me, I break the seal.

Dear James,

I know you've been to the woods and seen our cemetery. You can feel it, can't you—the great power of nature? How magical it is. How much it can give. How much it can take. You don't have much time. The Blood Moon is approaching. The forest is about to come to life.

Will you come forth and present yourself—willingly? Are you courageous enough? Do you have what it takes to save us all?

The Keeper

Shaking, I set the letter aside.

"James, I'm scared," Ava whimpers.

"Me too," I tell her. Then I put everything away quickly. Even my sandwich goes in the refrigerator, because I can't imagine eating anything right now. Every nerve in my body is quivering.

Upstairs, I watch Ava stop at her door and stare down at the doorknob without reaching for it. Standing beside her, Baxter wags his tail and whines. Ava strokes his fur and looks back at me.

"It's going to be okay," I tell her in a whisper. "We still have two more days. We'll figure this out."

Ava nods. "Do you think we should wake them up?" she asks. "Show them the letter. Tell them what happened down there?"

"They'll just get upset at us. Think it's another prank."

CHAPTER 14

After spending all morning researching nature and black magic on my father's computer in the den, Ava and I are getting nowhere. Baxter starts to whine that he wants to go for a walk, and I reach down to pet him.

"You had your morning walk," I tell him.

"Baxter, don't be a brat," Ava says, because she's a little frazzled. So, Baxter goes into the hallway and comes back with his leash in his mouth.

Laughing, I take the leash away from him and put it on the floor beside me. "No means no."

Baxter stares at it and whines. Then, because we are busy trying to see if there is any information about sorcerers in Oregon, Baxter gets up and leaves. He wanders out of the den and rushes up the stairs. I figure he's going to lie down on his doggy bed in Ava's room. But something else is going on, because we can hear him walking back and forth up there.

Ava gets up and looks out into the hall. "Baxter?" she calls after him. "What do you think he's doing up there?"

"I don't know," I tell her as I type in the words *covens in Oregon* and click on Images. The pictures that pop up make me jump back from the screen, and I sit up straight and look more closely at the pictures.

"Umm, Ava?" I call out to her. "Have you seen this?"

Ava puts her finger to her lips and grins at me. "Shh! I'm gonna go sneak up on him . . . see what he's doing."

"Forget that," I tell her. "You've got to see this."

Ava frowns and comes around the desk to look at the screen. "What in the world . . . It's not real! Is that real?"

"It's some kind of tradition up here," I tell her as I click on a website and read all about it. "They call it the Witch Paddle. Every Halloween, people all over Oregon get all dressed up and stand on their paddleboards to ride around on the surface of the water. Isn't that cool?"

Ava takes the mouse and clicks on picture after picture of people dressed as everything from old fashioned Pilgrim witches to modern warlocks. "Oregonians are so strange," Ava says.

"Not any stranger than us. Remember Ita and her stories of brujos and brujas living out in the woods of San Vicente, where she grew up? Look at that one paddling around with his skeleton dog howling at the moon. It's a statue, I think."

"I like Halloween, but that creeps me out," Ava whispers.

"Aww, come on," I say. "I can totally see myself dressing up like that with Baxter."

"Don't you dare!" Ava says. "Baxter's my dog. I decide what he's going to be for Halloween."

Just then, Baxter comes walking into the den carrying his torn Spiderdog costume in his mouth. "Well, look at that," I tell Ava, who's got her back to him. "I think someone's decided what he wants to wear."

"Baxter!" Ava hollers. "What are you doing with that? That's a horrible costume. Give it to me. Trust me—you never want to wear that. Ever again!"

"He's desperate for a walk," I tell her, because I think Baxter remembers the walks he's taken in that old harness I used to hold up his spider legs. So, I pick up Baxter's leash and put it on him. "Come on. It's time we took a break, anyway."

"Seriously, though," Ava says as we head out the door with our rain jackets on because the sky is gray and my weather app says there's a 70 percent chance of rain today. "Don't you think it's strange, how people like dressing up as witches out here? I think there's something there."

"Maybe," I say. "Or maybe it's just a coincidence."

"You know what they say!" Ava steps off the driveway and we head down Pine Circle.

"There are no coincidences."

"Exactly," Ava says. "If only there was someone we could trust. Someone we could ask about the letters."

We walk farther down and wait for Baxter to finish doing his business with his leg up against the bushes. Up in the sky, we see a bigger flock of black birds making wide, angled circles on the other side of Pine Circle.

"More cuervos," Ava says.

"A lot more." I pull up my phone and start taking pictures. But it's no use. The pictures come out all blurry. I can't get a good shot because the birds are too far away.

"Let's get closer," Ava says, and I nod.

Following the big flock of birds, we round Pine Circle and head up to the pond. Ava stops and points to the community garden. "Is that Mr. Morris?" she asks.

"It is," I say as I watch Mr. Morris hauling a watermelon up into his arms and walking to Betty's car. "Should we . . ."

"Help him?" Ava asks, stretching the words out so that I know this is part of our investigation. "We need to. We don't have a lot of time left."

"What are you two up to?" Mr. Morris says when he sees us coming over.

"Just walking Baxter," Ava says. "What are you going to do with all those watermelons?"

"Oh, I'm taking them back to the house," Mr. Morris says as he puts the green-striped melon in the trunk. "Betty puts them in special summertime crates, and delivers them to everyone in the neighborhood. It's kind of a tradition for her."

"Well, that's nice," I say. "So, you do it every year?"

Mr. Morris walks over and puts two more watermelons in the trunk. "It's our contribution to the community."

"Can we lend a hand?" Ava asks. "You look like you could use some help."

I look down at Baxter.

"Is it okay if we let him walk around?" I ask. "He already went number one, back there. So, I think he'll be okay in the garden."

As we go back and forth, filling up Betty's trunk, a truck comes around the bend. It slows down and comes to a stop in front of us. I look up and see Jack grinning at me from inside the cabin.

"Hey!" he yells. Then he opens the door and jumps out. "What are you two doing out here?"

"Just being a good neighbor," I say. "What about you? Why aren't you out playing?"

Jack shrugs. "I was helping my dad haul some old things to the thrift store," he says, pointing his thumb back at his father, who is out of his truck and heading toward us.

"Looks like you're all full over there, Morris," Mr. Harvey says. "Do you want to load the rest of these into my pickup? It would go much faster. One trip, and we'd be all done."

Mr. Morris stands up. He lifts his arm and wipes his brow with the cuff of his shirt. As he does, he peeks over at Mr. Harvey discreetly from behind his arm. Then he puts his gloved hands on his back and twists and stretches with a grunt. "Thank you. I'd be very grateful."

With all five of us working together, we finish picking up all the watermelons in no time at all. Feeling guilty about suspecting that Mr. Harvey might be the Keeper, I jump in the back of his truck with Ava, Jack, and Baxter for the short ride up the hill to Mr. Morris's house.

"Well, look at that," Betty says when the garage door opens, and she comes out of the shadows. Her blonde hair is tied up in a messy bun, and she's wearing a blue-jean jumper. "It's bigger than last year's harvest!"

"Yup," Mr. Morris says. "I think we'll have some left over."

"Oh, gosh," Betty says. "What should we do with the surplus?"

"I can take some into Portland," Mr. Harvey says. "Donate them to the food bank when I go back to work on Monday. They'll be glad to take them."

Betty smiles. "That would be great."

"Let's get them in here," Mr. Morris says, looking up at the sky. "It's going to start raining soon."

With Betty's help, we unload all the watermelons, stacking them up in shallow crates all along the wall of the garage. Baxter sniffs every crate as we fill it, and when we're done, Mr. Morris gives Ava the smallest watermelon to take home with her.

"Really?" Ava asks as she hugs the cute little watermelon in her arms like it's one of her dolls. "It's so pretty. I'll make a respectful fruit salad with it! Because our Ita always said we have to respect where our food comes from by using it to make beautiful meals."

"That's so true. I think I'll make a *respectful* fruit salad too," Betty says, and she takes a watermelon and starts to go into her house.

"Well, thanks for all your help, Harvey," Mr. Morris says as he walks out of the garage with the rest of us trailing behind him.

"You look parched," Betty says, looking at Ava's flushed cheeks. "Why don't you come in and have some fresh lemonade. I made it this morning."

Ava grins. "That sounds good."

Mr. Harvey walks to his truck and jumps in while Jack lingers in the driveway with us. Just as I'm about to walk around the house with Ava, I notice Betty's car is still running.

"Wait!" I call out. "Mr. Morris, you left your keys in the car."

"Did I?" Mr. Morris starts patting his pants pockets. "Well, I'll be darned. I sure did."

Thinking that this is a great opportunity to take one last peek around Mr. Morris's garage, I turn and head back to it. But as I approach, a gust of wind rushes up from behind me. It presses against me, almost sweeping me forward. At the same time, I hear a loud popping sound.

Pruuuuuuuuump!

A wire unravels and the garage door comes falling down.

Craaaack!

It slams violently in front of me.

It would have gotten me, except that Ava drops her baby watermelon and grabs my shirt. She pulls me so hard, I fall backward and land safely on my butt in the driveway. The door hits Ava's watermelon instead, busting it open and slicing it in half, like a dull guillotine.

"Whoa!" Jack hollers as he watches a piece of split watermelon spin on its bottom until it's sitting up, wobbling in front of us, its juicy guts splattered all over the gray concrete. "That was . . ."

". . . Intense," I whisper because I can feel my heartbeat drumming savagely inside my chest, and every muscle in my body is quivering. My knees and legs feel too weak to walk. So, I sit there completely in shock.

Mr. Morris stares down at me. His eyes are full of something strange. Something like fear. Or pain. And he looks like he's lost his ability to speak. "I'm . . . I'm . . . so . . . so sorry. I don't know how that happened."

"Are you okay?" Mr. Harvey asks, rushing up the driveway. "Everyone all right?"

"I'm okay," I tell him. "I'm not hurt. Ava . . ."

"Saved your life!" Jack exclaims, reaching down to give me a hand up.

I stand and dust myself off. Ava throws her arms around me. She doesn't say anything, but I can feel her little body shaking as she clings to my midriff.

"Don't be upset. I told you, I'm fine. I'm fine," I keep telling her, even though I'm shaking as much as she is, and it feels like I'm not holding her as much as we're holding each other up. "Come on. Let's go home. Okay?"

Ava lets me go and wipes the tears out of her eyes. "Yes. Home," she whispers.

"Dude. You're lucky!" Jack shakes his head and looks back at the busted watermelon as we walk down the driveway. "That could have been your skull!"

CHAPTER 15

Instead of talking about our investigation, Ava is very quiet when we get home. I figure three letters and three near accidents is just too much for her to discuss right now. I understand. It's almost too much for me. But I can't cower away and give up. I have to find out who is sending those letters. My life, and maybe even my whole family's lives, depends on it.

I decide to search for details about the children's deaths on my phone. I want to see if they had accidents like mine. Ava sits at my computer and researches urban legends, hauntings, and strange occurrences in Oregon, because she just knows there are supernatural forces at work here.

I believe she's onto something. The more I think about it, the more I am convinced the wind was blowing hard every time I got a letter or had an accident. I can't be sure, because my Ita used to say memory is a funny thing. The mind fills in gaps when there is information missing. That's why we made all those videos and uploaded them up to the cloud. So her stories and consejos wouldn't get all messed up in our heads because we were too sad or too upset after she was gone.

"Are you two all right?" my mother asks when we are too quiet at dinner.

I smush the garlic-mashed potatoes on my plate and push them away from my chicken. Mom doesn't like it when I get picky, so I don't say anything about it anymore. But I really hate it when my food items touch each other on the plate, especially when I've had a really bad day, like today. "I'm fine," I tell her.

"Fine," my father says. "Sounds like someone is not looking forward to going back to school in a few weeks. Is that what's bothering you two? Did the summer just fly by?"

"No," I tell him. "I'm actually hoping . . ."

"Looking forward to it!" Ava says, pressing her lips together into what looks like a realistic smile. Only I know she's as stressed about the Keeper as I am. "James and I were talking about it today. How we can't wait to start having something to do all day."

"Awww . . . you're worried, aren't you?" My mother reaches over and pushes the hair off my forehead and tucks it behind my ears. Then she looks over at my father and says, "Hey, I know it's a weeknight, but how about if we go into town together—go see a movie or walk around that nice big rose garden they have up there in Portland. The roses are blooming right now. We could take some nice family pictures."

The thought of having to smile for pictures right now is too much, and I shift around uncomfortably in my chair.

"Maybe when the afternoon traffic rush is gone," my father says. "We can take in a movie. I don't think we can get pictures with the roses today. It'll be dark by the time we get there."

"I think we should just stay home," I say. "Just the four of us. All safe and sound on the couch—like cochinillas."

"I have a better idea," Ava says. "Why don't you two call in sick tomorrow? We can snuggle up in our colchas, stay up together, and watch movies all night. Just the four us. We can turn off all the lights and not answer the door."

"That's tempting," my father says. "But why wouldn't we answer the door?"

"Because it's family time," I say. "And Ita used to say family time is sacred. We shouldn't let anything interfere with it."

My mother pulls her napkin off her lap and smiles. "Well, I'm in," she says. "Classes haven't started yet. And I don't have any meetings tomorrow. So, technically, I don't have to be on campus until six, for the Gala. What about you, Chris? Can you take a day off so soon after starting this new job?"

My father thinks about it. "I wouldn't feel right doing it," he says. "But I can pull an all-nighter. I used to do it all the time when I was in college."

"You did not!" My mother, who met my father in college, laughs. "He used to fall asleep during our study sessions. It's okay. We'll let you take naps between movies."

So, that's how we all spend the last night before the Blood Moon—holed up together in the den with the lights on low, munching on churros and nuts, drinking chocolate de olla, and watching classics in front of the fireplace.

When I wake up at eleven, a little confused about how I got up to my room, Ava is standing over my bed.

"Hey, you wanna go to the library with me?" she asks. She looks ready to go, all zipped up in her rain jacket.

"The library?" I ask. "What library?"

"The university library," Ava says as she crosses the room. "I told Mom I wanted to go. She thought it was a great idea. We're going to eat together in the cafeteria."

"So, you'll be there all afternoon?" I ask as I look out the window at the dark, drizzly day. "Why?"

Ava's eyes soften. "I'm worried about you. The Blood Moon's tonight, and you keep having all these accidents."

"But why the library?"

"I read the letters again. And I want to research this house," she says. "To see if any of those kids used to live here."

"That's actually a good idea," I say, running my fingers through my hair because I haven't slept long enough, and I have a small headache.

"Yeah. I have a good feeling about this." Ava takes my hand and pulls on it. "Come on. Get dressed. Mom says we're leaving in fifteen minutes."

"I can't be ready in fifteen minutes," I tell her. "You go. I want to go to Betty's house and see if I can talk to Mr. Morris."

Ava drops my hand. "Mr. Morris!" she cries. "Why?"

I pull the covers off and throw my legs over the side of the bed. "I know it's weird." I lean over and look under the bed for my slippers. "But he used to patrol the forest at night, remember, so he might know something about that old cemetery out there."

"You almost had an accident at his house! What if he's . . ."

I push my feet into my slippers and stand up. Ava moves out of the way, and I go look at the letters again. "I have to talk to him," I tell her. "The last letter says, *'The forest is about to come to life,'* and that's happening tonight. We don't have any more time to waste."

"Yes, but . . ."

"We don't have any more time to waste," I repeat.

"But you'll be careful, right?" Ava asks. "You won't go out there with him. You're just going to talk to him. At his house. When Betty's there."

"Yes," I say. "Don't worry. I know how to take care of myself."

"Okay," Ava says. "I'll go to the library and you'll talk to Mr. Morris and we'll meet back here this afternoon, to talk about what we discover. Okay?"

"Sounds like a plan," I tell her.

Even though it's drizzling heavily, at exactly twelve thirty, I pull my rain jacket hood over my head and walk out the back door. Because I have to cut across the muddy field behind our house,

I can't ride my bike. But it's okay because I don't want the chain to get all rusty from the rain.

As I look up, I notice the sky above is full of big black birds again. There's even more of them today, and they are absolutely everywhere. They're cawing loudly and soaring so low in the sky above our neighborhood, I don't have to take pictures to get a good look at them with my scope as they circle around in their own little orbits, moving farther and farther south as they go. Fascinated, I walk past Mr. Morris's house and keep going, moving along with the birds as I follow the tree line.

"James! James!"

I turn around and see Mrs. Martin is calling to me from her house. I pull the hood of my jacket back a bit and look across the field at her. She's standing on her back porch, smiling pleasantly, and waving for me to come over. I don't want to be mean and just ignore her, even though I want to get back to Mr. Morris's house as soon as possible. After all, Mrs. Martin does make those special baseball-shaped cookies for us. So, I drop the scope and run toward her.

Her backyard is not all sodded like ours is, and I almost slip when I hit a muddy patch on the ground. But I catch myself before I fall and walk carefully over the squishy area to her back porch.

"Can I help you?" I ask, squinting because the rain is getting caught in my eyelashes.

"As a matter of fact, you can," she says. "Thank you for coming over. Please, get out of the rain."

"Thank you," I say, stepping onto the porch and shaking the drizzle off my hood and shoulders. "What can I do for you?"

Mrs. Martin tightens her lips and raises her hands apologetically. "Well, my daughter Madison is driving in for a visit with her family and their big Saint Bernard, so I've been cleaning the dog kennel all morning." She opens the door and keeps talking as we walk inside. "But I just can't bend over to scrub that stubborn crud out of those corners. And Mr. Martin, well, he went into town with Beth to pick up some groceries, so he's not here to help me. Is that something you could do for me? I couldn't pay you in cash, but I just baked two lemon meringue pies. You could take one home to your family, if you like."

"Oh, no, no. You don't need to pay me." I wave a hand in the air, to let her know that's a silly idea. My parents would be horrified if I took payment for helping someone in need. Especially someone who brought over a basket of scones for our family.

"Well, thank you, James." Mrs. Martin's house smells like ammonia, and something else, something I can't quite place, something warm and stinky, something other than lemon meringue pie. "The kennel's down in the basement. Follow me. Right this way."

I've never been in Beth's house. But I'm still surprised by the layout when I walk through it. The kitchen is small, with windows and a bright overhead light, but the rest of the house is a dark, smelly web of hallways and doors and stairs.

"Wow," I say. "This house is like a maze."

"I'm sorry," Mrs. Martin says. "I know. It needs an update,

189

but Robert and I live on a small budget. This house has been in our family for generations, and though we try to keep it up, we can't afford to remodel. It would cost more than the house is worth to renovate everything."

I blush, thinking about our more modern, beautiful house, with its high windows, sunny rooms, and tall ceilings. "No, no," I say. "I wasn't saying you should do anything to it. It's part of your heritage. You shouldn't have to change it."

"Thank you, James," Mrs. Martin says, smiling primly. "I'm so glad you came over to help. You have no idea what this means to me, to us."

Mrs. Martin turns left. She picks up a pair of gloves from a table and hands them to me. And when I stand there, staring at the giant, iron, cage-like kennel in her basement, Mrs. Martin picks up a bottle of disinfectant. She tests it, spraying it in front of my face. The scent of ammonia reaches my nose and awakens my senses. I shake my head to clear my mind.

"That's a kennel?" I ask, looking back at the massive cage.

Mrs. Martin scrunches her nose and giggles. "We love our daughter's Saint Bernard. He's part of the family. Robert and I didn't want him to get all twisted up like a pretzel in one of those small wire things they sell at the pet store. So, Robert made this one especially for him a few years ago."

"I bet he loves having the extra room," I say, and I pull on the gloves.

"Oh, yes." Mrs. Martin hands me a cleaning rag and the disinfectant. "Bubba loves his home away from home. I spruce it up for him. Toss in all kinds of pillows and a big, bulky blanket, and he's in heaven."

"I'm sure," I say. "I'd like it too, if I was a dog."

"Are you ready?" Mrs. Martin asks, and she opens the door to the kennel and steps inside, hunching over slightly and walking forward to show me where she needs me to scrub. "See here? I just can't get down there and dig into those small crevices anymore. My knees just won't let me."

"Oh, that's easy," I say, dropping to my hands and knees and spraying the corner with the disinfectant, making sure I get enough of the ammonia on it to soften up the gunk in the corners. "I'll be done in no time."

Mrs. Martin exits the cage as I start to scrub.

I hear a loud clinking sound and turn around.

"Take all the time you need," Mrs. Martin says, smiling sweetly at me.

Suddenly, her smile turns downward, and she sighs as she locks the door on the kennel.

"What are you doing?" I ask, stopping mid-scrub to look at her as she walks away.

But instead of answering me, Mrs. Martin starts to climb up the stairs. I drop the bottle of disinfectant and rush to rattle the door of the kennel.

"Mrs. Martin?" I yell. "What are you doing? Let me outta here! I need to go home!"

"Robert!" Mrs. Martin calls out as she opens the door at the top of the stairs. "Come down here!"

. Thinking fast, I reach into the left pocket of my cargo pants. But when I try to turn on my phone, it's totally black. Shocked, I shake my phone and try to start it again, but it's no use. Even though I had only charged it an hour before, it's dead as a brick now.

Mr. Martin follows his wife down the stairs. He walks toward me. With his red hair combed back smoothly over his ears, he looks like he was just getting ready for a special occasion. I slide my phone back into my pocket quietly.

"Well, look at that!" Mr. Martin's beady green eyes glimmer in the musty basement. "You captured the *courageous young-blood* all by yourself. Congratulations, my dear. You've secured the posterity of our community. I'll go let the others know."

Youngblood? Courageous? My stomach drops to my feet.

"Wait!" I call after Mr. Martin, who has turned around and is heading back to the stairs. "Wait! Wait! I'm not *courageous*! You have the wrong kid."

Mrs. Martin crinkles her little snub nose as she looks back at me with her sparkling blue eyes. "Oh, we think you're very brave, James," she says, and she giggles and shakes her head.

My stomach hurts, and I feel like throwing up. But I can't let them leave. Not before they release me. "I don't think—I know I'm not the *youngblood* you're looking for," I tell Mrs. Martin. "Trust me. I'm the least courageous person in the whole wide world."

"Oh, but you *are*. You are everything we could have hoped for and so much more," Mrs. Martin says, turning around at the bottom of the stairs to look back at me.

Mr. Martin raises his hand and shows me his thumb and two fingers. "Three times we tried to stop you, and three times you persisted. Don't sell yourself short, young man. You answered the call and proved yourself worthy. Even when we sent Ms. Phillips after you . . . you didn't quit. Scared as you were, you pressed on!"

"Wait," I say. "Who's *we*? Is one of you . . . the Keeper?"

"Oh, gosh, no," Mr. Martin says. "We're just doing our part, helping the Keeper restore balance again."

"And the Keeper told you to lock me up?" I ask.

At my words, Mrs. Martin raises her hands in front of her face and makes tiny clapping sounds with her fingertips. "Yes, sweet boy. *You* are the brave one we've all been waiting for!"

"Come, dearest. We can't waste one more minute," Mr. Martin tells his wife. "We have to prepare for the sacrifice!"

Sacrifice!

The word brings forth images of covens and sorcery and flames leaping up into the air somewhere deep in the woods. The whole thing sends shivers down my spine and, feeling dizzy, I drop to my knees. Then I grab the iron bars of the kennel door and look up at my captors.

"Sacrifice?" I call out to them as they rush up the creaky stairs. "What do you mean, sacrifice? Come back! You can't leave me here!"

When the door closes behind them, I rattle the cage again and again, pulling and pushing with all my might. But nothing works. I am absolutely and most definitely trapped! Desperately, I throw my weight against the front of the cage, to see if I can lift it off the ground and topple it over. But the kennel is solid and has no give. I even lie on my back and try to kick the door open. But the door is too sturdy, and I end up with painful, throbbing feet, a racing heart, and sweat gushing down my face and neck.

Scared out of my mind, I lie back and look all around me, to see if there is anything nearby that I can reach and pull into the kennel to help me break out. As I sit there, for what feels like hours, listening to the horrible cawing of birds landing on the lawn and walking around the Martins' yard, I wonder if I am ever going to see Ava and my parents again.

I sit against the far end of the cage and let the tears roll down my face unashamed. I cry for myself, for Ava, for my parents. I even cry for my friends, Beto and Mike, who will be so sad when they find out I'm never coming back. But most of all, I cry for my Ita. Because she always believed in me. She had such high hopes for me, and now I'm not going to accomplish my dreams the way she always said I would.

Ignoring the thunder and the caw, caw, cawing that is getting louder and louder outside the window, I keep wishing I had done everything differently. I wish I hadn't followed Mrs. Martin down into the basement. I wish I had just gone to the library with Ava instead of heading out on my own. I wish my parents had believed me when I showed them the letters. But, more than anything, I wish we had never moved to this rainy, miserable place!

Spotting a mop sitting against the wall to my left, I reach out until my fingers make contact with the dirty threads of yarn attached to the head. I pull on those mechas until the mop drops. Then I latch on to it and pull it inside the kennel. I am trying to figure out what I can do with it when I hear a very bad imitation of a screech owl coming from outside the window beside the kennel.

Ava?

Yes! I tell myself. Because that is the sound of my sister making the secret owl call our Ita taught us since we were small, the sound I recorded at the hospital, the sound I have heard many times before—Lechuza's Song—the song of hope and love! She finally got it right!

Standing up, I use the mop's handle to hit the crusty, painted-over latch on the window. I push and prod until it finally gives way and flips over. Once that's open, I use the tip of the handle to push the window up, one creaky, slow, grumpy inch at a time—until the window is open wide enough that I can feel a cool, moist draft coming into the dark, damp basement.

The sound of my sister's owl screech gets closer and closer, and I lean against the cage and call out to her. "Ava! Ava!" I cry out loud enough for her to hear me, but hopefully not loud enough to be heard upstairs by the Martins. "I'm over here! In Mrs. Martin's basement!"

"James? Is that you?" Ava creeps over and peeks into the

window, lowering her face close to the ground, so she can look inside better. "Are you in there, James?"

"Yes," I whisper. "You've got to get me out of here, Ava. I'm locked up in a cage."

"A cage?" Ava's eyes open wide in the darkness, and I can hear it in her voice: She is just as scared as I am.

My sister uses all her strength to pull up the creaky, swollen window, and when it's all the way open she climbs into the basement. Because the window is pretty high, she anchors her leg over a wingback chair and pulls it over, so she doesn't have to fall so far down from the window ledge. Landing on the chair, Ava takes a deep breath before she sits up and comes to check on me.

"How did you find me?" I ask her as she messes with the latch on the gate.

Ava gives up on the latch and sighs. "Well, first, I saw all the birds, and I thought they must be over here for a reason. Then I saw your shoe prints in the mud, and that's when I was sure you had come this way. How did you end up in here?" she asks as she grabs the bars and tests the door of the kennel.

"It's a long story," I say. "Can you find something to help me break off this lock? Something big and heavy, something I can hit it with."

Ava walks around the room, looking through boxes and shelves, but before she can find anything the door flies open, and the Martins come rushing down the stairs. "Well, look at that," Mrs. Martin says, turning her glimmering eyes to Ava. "We have a two-for-one special!"

Ava raises the spatula she's pulled out of a box up in the air, like it's a weapon.

"Run!" I scream.

My sister jumps to her left and sprints. She climbs over the wingback chair and hides behind an old armoire. But the Martins flank her, and before she can scream, or run, or do anything to defend herself, Mr. Martin grabs her. Then Mrs. Martin puts one arm around my sister's shoulders and a hand over her mouth, so she can't scream.

"Open the cage," Mrs. Martin orders, and Mr. Martin unlocks the kennel.

I try to push my way out, but Mr. Martin shoves the struggling Ava into the kennel so forcefully that my sister kicks me instead of him.

"I'm sorry," Ava cries into my shoulder when I reach out to hold her. "I'm sorry, James."

"Don't be sorry," I say. "This is my fault. Okay? I'm the one who got us trapped in here."

"No," Ava says. "I'm sorry I kicked your face."

"It's all right. It's okay," I whisper, and I rock her back and forth, because she's crying like a baby, and I don't know what else I can do for her. "We're going to be okay. I won't let them hurt you. I promise."

After the Martins leave to go *talk* upstairs, Ava calms down.

She pulls away from me, wipes the tears off her cheeks and the mucus off her nose. "This is crazy! I thought Beth said her mom didn't believe in all this stuff?" Then she hiccups. "Wait. Do you think they're trying to help? Did they put us in here . . . to protect us?"

"No. They're not. They kept calling me *youngblood* and *courageous*," I tell her. "Which means . . ."

Ava's eyes narrow. "One of them wrote the letters! But why? What do they want from us?"

I swallow hard as I think about what they said. "I don't want to be dramatic," I tell her. "But I think they want to *sacrifice* me."

Saying it out loud makes it real, and suddenly I feel faint. My hands begin to tremble. And I feel sick to my stomach.

"Don't get upset." Ava wraps her arms around my shoulders. "You'll see. We'll get out of here before they can sacri . . ."

Angry, I reach up and rattle the cage. Then I look at my sister. "What's in your backpack?"

CHAPTER 16

As it turns out, there's nothing I can use in Ava's backpack. "I'm sorry," she says. "I wasn't ready for this."

"I don't think anyone could be ready for this," I tell her.

Ava's about to zip up her backpack, but then she changes her mind. She reaches into a pocket, deep inside, and pulls out a handful of newspaper printouts.

"I almost forgot. I found this at the library," she says, handing me one of the printouts. "You're not going to believe it. But our house burned down a hundred years ago. And a boy died in the fire."

I look at the picture of the ruined house and read the headline, *Young Man Perishes in Home Fire!* "That's—"

"—horrible, I know," Ava whispers. "But that's not all."

Skimming the newspaper article makes me shiver. "Not all? What could be worse than a boy burning to death in our home?"

Ava hands me a second, third, and fourth printout. "Stephanie has it all wrong. Many bad things have happened over the years in this neighborhood—a whole lot of strange 'accidents' have happened in this village, James." Ava uses her air quotes to emphasize the word *accidents*.

"Like what?" I ask. My heart is racing so hard, I can feel it practically bruising my lungs.

"Well, read!" Ava points to the headlines. "Falls. Drownings. Disappearances. Terrible things happen to children who live here. And guess what? They all lived on Pine Circle. That is *not* a coincidence!"

I read and reread the printouts. And Ava is right. In front of me are stories of how different children from our neighborhood have suffered some kind of horrible accident.

"Well, that's . . . hard to read." I hand Ava back the papers, while I take a moment to think.

"We have to get out of here," Ava says, putting the papers back in the backpack and scanning the room around us.

But no matter what we try, we can't find a way out. We spend a good amount of time taking turns trying to pick the lock with one of the barrettes holding up Ava's braids.

When the Martins return, Mr. Martin comes right up to the cage to stare at us. He cocks his head when he sees us holding on to each other inside the huge kennel.

"And how are you two doing in there?" he asks as he leans over and smiles at us. "Is there anything we can get you?"

"You can let us go," I say.

"We won't tell anyone you did this," Ava says, shifting beside me, ready to spring up into action. "We'll just go home and pretend this never happened."

Mr. Martin looks at his wife and says, "The weather is misbehaving again. It's a good thing Beth went to stay with your sister in Portland. It's nice and clear up there. We should start the furnace. We don't want any harm to come to them before the ritual tonight."

He walks over to the other end of the basement and pries opens a dark iron door to a small oven built into the wall.

"Furnace?" My voice sounds squeaky, like the sound a mouse makes when it's caught in one of those vicious glue traps, and I clear my throat.

"Can you do something about that window?" Mr. Martin asks. "I can't stand all that noise out there. I swear, it's getting worse."

Mrs. Martin reaches into a box, pulls out a crowbar, and closes the window, using the hook at the end to bring down the creaky frame.

"That's better," Mr. Martin whispers. Then he takes a chair and sits down in front of the kennel. "May we look through your bag?" he asks Ava.

"No! It's mine." Ava frowns and hugs her backpack close to her chest. But Mrs. Martin puts her hand through the iron bars, reaches far into the kennel, and grabs the strap of the backpack. Then she yanks and twists and turns and gets into a tug-of-war with Ava until she threads the backpack through the iron bars.

"Here you go," she says as she hands Ava's backpack to her husband.

Mr. Martin takes Ava's belongings out of her bag, one thing at a time, throwing them into the flames of the furnace. Then he unzips the front pocket, pulls out the library printouts, and reads through them. "I think you need to see this."

"They know!" Mrs. Martin cries as she reads over her husband's shoulder.

"That's right," Ava says. "We figured it out. We know everything."

"Everything?" Mr. Martin laughs. Then he turns to his wife and says, "Well, that's a mouthful. Isn't it?"

"They're just kids. They always think they know everything!" Mrs. Martin says. But even though she tries not to show it, I can tell she's a little unsettled. The flames from the furnace dance over her worried face as she feeds the fire.

Thinking about everything I've ever read and heard about kidnappings, I remember one very important thing a policeman said in an interview on TV: You should always try to connect with your abductors. You should speak to them about your family, your friends, your pets, anything that might make them see you more as a human being. But you must do it right away.

This part is critical. This can save your life.

"I know your ancestors left you this house," I tell Mrs.

Martin. "It's part of your heritage. Heritage is important to us too. That's why it was hard to move here. To leave all our friends back in Texas."

Ava frowns at me. I give her a knowing look, and she raises her eyebrows and nods.

"That's right," Ava chimes in. "And our grandmother Ita, my mother's mother, she used to say culture is important too. She came from Mexico. She's gone now. But she left us her way of thinking about life."

"We still have her consejos—her advice," I say. "We didn't inherit a house from her, but we inherited her language."

"And food. We inherited her recipes. Thanks to her, my mother and father make all kinds of homemade Mexican food for us," Ava says, because now she sees exactly what I'm trying to do. "Do you like Mexican food?"

"Okay, enough of this nonsense," Mr. Martin says. Then he looks at the printouts again.

"I see what you're trying to do. She's a smart cookie, isn't she? I always advocated for her," Mrs. Martin whispers as she continues to read over her husband's shoulder. "Do you think they'll let us sacrifice her too? It might lengthen the time between rituals."

"I doubt if sacrificing her would make any difference," Mr. Martin says. Then he gets up, hands the printouts to his wife, and tells her to throw the papers in the furnace. "Besides, the rules are clear. One sacrifice every twenty-five years. A *courageous youngblood*. Tried and true. Nothing more. Nothing less."

"Why are you doing this?" I ask when I watch the flames in the furnace flicker and flutter and devour the evidence Ava collected at the library. "We've done nothing to you. We're just kids."

Mr. Martin looks back at us shivering inside the kennel and shakes his head. "We'll have to do something with her, get rid of her—eventually. But for now, we have to make sure our *courageous youngblood* stays warm and safe. Give him plenty of water and feed him fresh fruits and nuts. No more sweets. We need to maintain his vitality."

Then he starts heading toward the stairs.

One sacrifice every twenty-five years.

A courageous youngblood.

Tried and true.

Nothing more.

Nothing less.

What kind of people are these? I ask myself as I try to figure out what we need to do to get away from them. *Think! Think,* my mind says as I try to put it all together. Because I have so many questions. Why do these people think they have to do this? What was it the last letter said? *Will you come forth and present yourself—willingly? Are you courageous enough?*

"Oh, my God!" I scream—the words fly out of my mouth before I can stop them. "This isn't going to work!"

"What?" Ava asks.

"What's going on?" Mr. Martin asks, turning around to look at us again.

"You can't do this," I tell him. "The letter spelled it out, loud and clear."

"Ah, yes, the letter. That's why the Keeper sent them, to test you," Mrs. Martin explains as she grazes the iron bars with her fingertips, like the kennel is some kind of musical instrument only she knows how to play.

"Of course. You needed to find someone to sacrifice," I say, drawing away from the kennel door and stepping backward, careful to keep Ava safe behind me. "Someone dumb enough to fall for your tricks."

"Tsk-tsk. Not dumb." Mr. Martin shakes his finger at me. "Don't sell yourself short, young man. The Keeper had to find someone brave—someone *courageous* enough not to give up when things got tough. Someone worthy of the sacrifice."

Mr. Martin's smile reveals long, glinting canines that graze the corners of his lips. And I wonder why I hadn't noticed them before. But he's no werewolf. He's something worse—he's a murderer! And I can see he's been toying with me this whole time.

"Well, you picked the wrong kid," I tell him. "You just don't know it yet."

Mr. Martin's face changes. His eyebrows furrow over his narrowing eyes, like he's starting to rethink this whole thing. "You don't know what you're talking about."

"Yes, I do," I say as Mr. Martin moves slowly toward the door of the cage. "We were right all along. You're a coven! And you're using black magic! And those children, the children who died in

205

those accidents, did *they* come to you willingly?"

"It is the decree," Mrs. Martin says. "Though there has been—one exception. But the sacrifice nearly undid the Keeper. Even after he recovered, he had a hard time restoring order to our environment."

"One exception?" I ask. "You mean the boy who burned in our house."

The Martins don't confirm it, but they don't have to. It's clear that's what they're talking about. Ava scoots behind me. She puts her hands around my waist and clings to me. "Why would you do that? Why would you kill innocent children?" she asks.

"Power. Prosperity. Peace of mind." Mr. Martin comes so close, I can smell his foul breath all the way inside the cage. "Every twenty-five years, during the Blood Moon, the Keeper and the Founding Families must sacrifice a child. Through this sacrifice, the Keeper gains control over the natural world."

Mrs. Martin stands beside her husband and looks quietly into the cage. Her hands folded in front of her as if in prayer, she looks like the kindest, gentlest mother. Only she's not kind! And she's not gentle!

"You don't know what it was like, before the sacrifices," Mrs. Martin whispers. "Our forefathers, the Founding Families of this town, were persecuted, criminalized, abused. That's why they left everything they loved and cared about behind and came to Oregon. They sacrificed everything to build this perfect community—so that their children and their children's children would live in abundance and prosperity—forever."

"Sacrifice everything," I say. "You mean children, don't you?"

"Mother Nature can be harsh . . . but, ultimately, she is the most generous of all forces," Mr. Martin explains. "If we please her, if we do right by her, she will take care of us for another generation. Because we willingly sacrifice a courageous young-blood, a child of our very own, a child we have taken into the very heart of our community, Mother Nature willingly lends us her divine protection."

"I know it's hard for you to understand our way of life," Mrs. Martin admits. "But it's a fair exchange. In order to provide for the ones *we* love, sacrifices have to be made. I'm sorry it's you, James. I really am, but you answered the call."

"I know," I tell her, standing up and grabbing the iron bars so that she can look into my eyes as I speak slowly, softly. "I did come into the house *willingly*. I even walked into this cage *will ingly*. But we won't go anywhere else with you—not willingly."

"You'll see," Ava says. "When you least expect it, we'll be gone."

"We're not letting you take us to the cemetery," I tell Mr. Martin. "That is where you make the sacrifices, isn't it? At the old cemetery?"

Mr. Martin smiles at his wife. "See? I told you. Clever *and* courageous!"

"So, what happened with that boy you burned in our house?" Ava asks. "Why didn't you take him to the cemetery?"

Mrs. Martin shrugs her shoulders. "We were running out of time."

"And now . . . well, now it's your turn," Mr. Martin says, his voice calm, almost . . . *resigned.* "I really am sorry it's you, James. You're so brave. Even when you don't want to be, you can't help it, can you? It's part of your nature. It's been a pleasure watching you live up to your potential."

As he turns away, Mr. Martin wipes a tear out of the corner of his eye. His honesty takes me by surprise, and I don't know how to react to him. I want to be mad, but I'm not sure how I feel. Angry? Upset? Desperate?

"No! Let him go!" Ava yells from behind me. "Sacrifice me! I'm *courageous* too!"

"You?" Mr. Martin stares at Ava, but only for a moment before he turns away. "No. That's not the way it works."

"You're smart and clever, I'll give you that." Mrs. Martin looks at my sister like she's disappointed with what she sees. "But James is the one we need. James answered the call. He faced his fears and didn't let our little 'accidents' stop him."

"Little accidents?" I ask. "You mean, the bookshelf?"

"And the tree!" Ava cries.

Mrs. Martin nods and smiles smugly. "Don't forget the garage door."

Mr. Martin lifts his hands high up into the air and says, "Only by taking the life force of a *courageous youngblood* can we begin to control the elements and ensure our safety and security for another twenty-five years. Thank you, James. Thank you for safeguarding our future!"

"Yes. Thank you, James," Mrs. Martin whispers. "Your sacrifice will be . . ."

" . . . remembered," Mr. Martin says.

"Celebrated!"

CHAPTER 17

The Martins leave the basement, and while they're gone, I notice that the sky outside the high window beside the kennel is getting darker and darker with every passing minute. But it isn't the time that is causing the change. The sun is still out. There is something darker, more frightening, happening out there.

From inside the kennel, I can hear birds cawing and cackling. And when I stand up and crane my neck, I see that a huge flock of the big black birds has begun to gather on the trees and shrubs of the Martins' backyard. There are hundreds and hundreds of them out there.

I see Mr. Martin trying to shoo them away by waving a broom at them, but they refuse to move. Instead of being intimidated, the birds flap their wings and raise their heads and cry into the air.

Kee-kaaw!

Kee-koow!

Kee-keew!

The black birds caw and caw, over and over again, getting louder and louder.

"What do you think it means?" Ava asks.

"I don't know," I say as I sit back down.

"I think they know the people in this house are pure evil," Ava whispers.

I don't want to be scared. But I am.

The Martins come back with food and beverages that they pass to us through the iron bars of the kennel. I take the water bottles, open one, and immediately hand it to Ava. Her cheeks are flushed, and I don't want her to pass out.

"Thank you," Ava says.

"You're welcome," Mrs. Martin says, smiling as she pushes a tiny box of raisins through the iron grate.

"She wasn't talking to you," I tell Mrs. Martin as I snatch the raisins out of her hand. "This isn't a 'thank you' kind of situation, so she wasn't thanking *you*. She was thanking *me*."

"Yeah. I wasn't talking to you." Ava glares at Mrs. Martin as she takes another swig of water.

The Martins ignore her as the birds begin letting out high-pitched cries. "Oh, Robert, isn't there something you can do?" she says. "Those things are driving me crazy!"

Mr. Martin picks up the bag of treats and hands them back to his wife. "You know how it is," he says. "The birds are just waking up from their long surrender. It's instinctual. But things will get back to normal tonight. You'll see, the sacrifice will give us control over them again."

"I'm hungry, and tired, and I just wanna go home," Ava whispers after the Martins go back upstairs. "What are we going to do, James?"

"Well, they're not keeping us in here much longer," I tell her. "The question is, how are we going to get away from them then?"

Ava stands up and scoots in beside me. "Do you remember that 'Stranger Danger' show we saw on TV last year? The police lady said you never, ever let them take you to the second location. So, whatever happens, we have to fight them."

"That's right," I tell her, trying to sound confident, even though I'm terrified.

"James? I'm really scared now." Ava leans into me. She hugs me around the waist. "It's all right to be scared, isn't it?"

I put my arm over her shoulders and pull her close to me. "Of course. Fear gives us courage when our knees are knocking."

Ava pulls her head back to look up at me. "Hey! That's what Ita used to say!"

The look in her eyes reminds me of the last time we watched one of Ita's videos together. "Remember what she said in that last video?" I ask her. "You're clever and I'm brave, but together . . ."

"Together, we can overcome any obstacle!" Ava grins and her eyes sparkle. "She did say that. I remember."

I let go of Ava and put my hand through the iron bars and point at a shelf. "See that box, over there? That's where Mrs.

Martin put down the crowbar."

"Yes." Ava nods. She lets go of my waist.

"And over there, to the left, that's a pretty big shovel," I say. "When they open the cage. I think we should both lunge forward and push them backward. To get them out of the way. Then we make a run for it, in opposite directions. I'll jump over the workbench and grab the shovel while you go around the table and grab the crowbar."

"Of course, but we have to get up the stairs," Ava says. "That's the real goal."

"That's right," I say. "But we'll be armed, if they try to grab us."

"Yes," Ava says. "I agree. We can't just let them take us. We can't go *willingly* . . ."

"Exactly. So, we have a plan then?" I ask her. "We lunge, push, rush, grab weapons, and run for the stairs."

"Yes," Ava says, and she opens another water bottle and drinks greedily from it. Then she keeps repeating the plan over and over again, out loud, like she's afraid to forget it. " . . . Lunge. Push. Rush. Grab. Stairs . . . Lunge, Push. Rush. Grab. Stairs . . . Lunge. Push. Rush. Grab. Stairs . . . Got it."

Ava sits on the floor and rests her back against the kennel again. Only this time, she unzips her rain jacket and starts to fan herself with her hand. "It's hot in here," she complains. "I wish they hadn't started that furnace."

After a while, the heat in the room starts to get to Ava and she lies down. I look at the birds outside. There are so many of them out there now. Though they are blocking the sun, I figure it's about four or five o'clock.

"Hey, did you bring your bike?" I ask Ava.

She shakes her head.

"That's okay," I say. "We can run home. It's not that far."

"I'm not feeling well," Ava whispers. She reaches out to take my hand and presses it against her forehead. "Do I have a fever?"

"You're okay. It's just really hot in here." I hold Ava's cold, clammy hand and try not to worry. "But don't fall asleep. I need you to jump into action when they come back. Okay? . . . *Lunge. Push. Rush. Grab. Stairs . . . Lunge, Push. Rush. Grab. Stairs.* Remember?"

"I remember," Ava says. "I'm just going to rest my eyes for a bit."

But even as I sit there, gripping my sister's limp hand in mine, and listening to the *Kee-kaaw! Kee-koow! Kee-keew!* of angry birds shrieking viciously outside the window, I can't help but worry. What if we're not strong enough? What if they bring others . . . No. I can't think like that.

We have to make it out of this alive.

CHAPTER 18

I am not sure how much time has passed, but when I open my eyes the room is dark, and the sound of the birds outside has stopped. Either the massive flock has left, or night has come, and they are roosting for the evening.

Whatever the reason for the darkness and the silence, I don't have time to figure it out, because when the Martins return, we can tell they are about to move us. Mr. Martin is unraveling a thick cord of rope and his wife is carrying a big roll of duct tape in her hands as they walk down the stairs.

"Get ready," I whisper, shaking Ava awake.

"*Lunge. Push. Rush. Grab. Stairs . . . Lunge. Push. Rush. Grab. Stairs . . . Lunge. Push. Rush. Grab. Stairs—*" Beside me, Ava repeats the plan like it's a prayer.

However, things never go my way. And our plan goes off track the minute Mr. Martin stands to the left of the kennel instead of standing directly behind or beside his wife, as I imagined he would when I put the plan together in my mind.

"Open the door," Mr. Martin tells his wife.

As Mrs. Martin fiddles with the lock, I turn to stare at Ava, to show her with my eyes that we are going to have to lunge separately.

But instead of changing the plan, I just take action.

"¡Águas!" I scream as I lunge forward.

"Arrgh!" Ava grunts as she rushes onward.

With both of us driving our shoulders into Mrs. Martin, she falls backward. Only, Mrs. Martin doesn't go down alone. She grabs my sister by the hair and pulls her down with her.

"Ahhhhh!" Ava screams as she struggles against Mrs. Martin.

I try to help, but her husband loops the rope around my arms and torso and tries to pull me up. As I fly backward, I see Ava open her mouth wide and bite down on Mrs. Martin's arm.

"Auuuugh!" Mrs. Martin howls as she lets go of my sister's hair to grab at her arm.

Ava scrambles up and runs off. Because she can't find the crowbar, she picks the spatula off the floor and turns around to face Mrs. Martin.

Mr. Martin tries to pull on the rope, but I untangle myself, scramble up, and lunge. I crash into him and we fall together, but Mr. Martin is strong. And he throws a second loop around me, making it hard for me to move. And when he pulls me up, I struggle to keep my balance.

Mrs. Martin gets up and has a standoff with Ava, who is holding the spatula in the air, ready to strike the wiry woman with it if she touches her again.

"Get her!" Mr. Martin screams as he pushes me toward the stairs. "Come on! We don't have all night. It's almost six already!"

Almost six!

Where do our parents think we are?

Mrs. Martin doesn't lunge at Ava, and Mr. Martin loses his patience and flings me sideways, so that I am forced to stumble toward his wife.

"Here," he says. "Hold him. I'll get her."

"No," Mrs. Martin says, and she starts walking slowly toward my sister.

Ava raises the spatula and strikes, but Mrs. Martin avoids the attack by putting her forearm in front of her. She grips my sister's arm and yanks the spatula out of her hands. "Come on. Let's go."

"Lead the way, my dear," Mr. Martin says, and he pulls me back so that I am out of his wife's way.

I twist and struggle against the rope, but Mr. Martin tightens his hold on it. He pushes me forward so that I fall in line behind Mrs. Martin as she hauls my sister up the stairs by the arm.

As I walk up behind them, I push my arms back and forth and side to side, until I feel the rope give way. Quickly, I pull it up and over my shoulders, loosening my arms enough to let me turn around and wrap myself around the wooden banister.

Using the force of my own body, I raise a leg and kick Mr. Martin in the stomach, hard.

He grunts and falls down the stairs, making a couple of overhead flips and landing at the bottom in what I can only describe as an old, crumpled churro.

I don't want to be proud of myself, but I am.

"Robert!" Mrs. Martin screams, and she lets go of Ava. She pushes me aside and rushes down the stairs to go check on her husband.

"Ohhhh! My back! My back!" Mr. Martin cries as he tries to move. "What have you done to my back?"

"¡Ándale! Go!" I yell, and Ava runs up the stairs quickly.

I follow her, taking the stairs two at a time, to catch up with her.

"Can you lock it?" I ask, winded by the effort of getting out of there before Mrs. Martin decides to come after us.

Ava turns the strange lock, and we hear it click. "Yes!"

"Okay, let's get out of here," I gasp.

"Whoa!" Ava says as we hurry through the maze of hallways and doors and stairs. "Which way is which?"

"I'm not sure," I say. "Just start opening doors, okay? We'll find the way out, eventually."

But when I open a door to my left, she stops and looks back at me.

I stick my head in and have to back off.

"Ewww. What's that smell?" I ask her, unable to hold back my disgust. The dark, shadowy room smells strongly of something old and gummy, something like turpentine.

"Incense?" Ava asks, and she steps away from the door.

"No, it's some kind of candle wax," I say because, from where I stand, I can see there are small black candles burning on the far end of the room. The flickering of all those flames is not enough to light the whole place, but it's enough to let us see that this is not a regular room. It looks a lot like the shrine at the Santuario de la Virgen de Guadalupe, where we used to attend church with our Ita when we visited her mother's gravesite in Piedras Negras, Coahuila. Only this shrine looks dark and dangerous.

"This is too creepy!" Ava says, and she turns away to leave.

"Hold on," I say, because something has caught my eye.

Beside the altar, I see a silky dark-green robe hanging from a hook. But what's important, what's caught my attention, is the semi-visible emblem stenciled onto the back.

"That looks like . . ." I go into the room and walk directly toward the robe. I reach up and pull on the sleeve so that the rest of the emblem is revealed to me.

"I don't understand." Ava's eyebrows furrow. "What is it?"

"Don't you see?" I ask, pulling the robe off the hook and showing it to her. "It's the seal that was on the letters!"

"We should take it," Ava says.

"Take it?"

"As evidence. For the police."

Then she says, "Wow, look at those." Ava points to the metal artwork hanging on the wall beside us. "They look like weapons."

"That's because they are," I tell her. "From a long time ago, I suspect."

Ava's eyes glisten as she stares up at the crooked, bent bows and barbed spears. "What are they doing here?"

Thinking about why the Martins own such creepy-looking weapons, I shudder involuntarily. "Come on. We shouldn't be in here."

"Wait!" Ava rushes over to a table on the left. She picks up a folded envelope and yells, "Jackpot!" before she folds it up and shoves it in her pocket.

At the same time, I notice a shiny black box sitting on the table where she found the envelope. I pick it up and examine it. There is a symbol carved on it too, but it's not exactly a match to the emblem on the letters and the robe. This is only one of the symbols from the four panels that complete the seal.

"You should take that too," Ava says. "It looks important."

I open the box, quickly flipping the lid up to reveal a crystal. The blue, gritty-looking rock sparkles and shimmers when I move the box side to side. So I grab the crystal and close the lid on the box quickly.

Just then, we hear a noise coming from somewhere in the house.

"They're out!" I say. "Come on. Let's get out of here!"

I toss the robe aside and shove the crystal into my pants

pocket. Then we rush down the hall, turn left at the corner, and run up a flight of stairs. And when we get to the end of the hall, we realize we are standing in the kitchen. Without wasting another minute, we throw the door open.

As we dart out of the back door, a swarm of birds caw, caw, caw and flap their wings as they take flight. Turning the gray sky above us almost black, they circle the house silently, like some kind of evil spirits. As we run, we hear a car driving down the slick road to our left, and we hide behind a bush. It drives by slowly, and we shiver and shake, because we can feel the danger that lies all around us.

By this point the Martins must have told *the others* that we've escaped. They'll be watching for us. So, we run across the field, in wet, mud-soaked sneakers and sopping socks. We can't let anyone see us. So, we have no other choice.

We have to cut through the woods!

CHAPTER 19

The dark, deep woods are eerie, and as Ava and I run through the shadows the branches of the old crooked trees threaten to reach out and grab us. I make my legs move faster and faster, pumping my arms to quicken my pace.

"You know we have to tell Mom and Dad," I say, talking quickly, because we're walking so fast, I can't hardly catch my breath.

Ava nods.

"Yes. Absolutely. I just hope they believe us. Wait. My side hurts. I have to rest a moment," she says, putting her hand on her side and taking a couple of deep breaths.

"They'll believe us," I say, leaning a hand on a tree to rest too, because my heartbeat is pounding louder than the rain on my head. "We have evidence. We can call the sheriff now."

"The sheriff?" Ava's eyes widen. "You think he can do anything?"

"Why wouldn't he?" I ask her.

"Well, you heard what Mr. Martin said . . . they control everything in their environment," Ava whispers, even though we seem to be alone in the woods.

I shake my head. "But they won't stay that way. Not if we don't let them get us."

"Which we won't." Ava digs her hands into the pockets of her rain jacket, looking up at the sliver of dark sky directly above us, and then she turns around to look back at me again.

"Are you okay?" I ask her.

Ava nods. "Yes. I just . . . well, I don't see anything. Do you?"

I lift my scope to my right eye and look up at the sky too, but there is no moon that I can see. And because of the dark clouds overhead, I can't see any stars either. So, I have no idea which way is which.

"Come on," I say, touching her elbow. "I think the house is this way."

Suddenly, we hear a noise. Something wild, something fierce, is heading our way. We stop. Freeze. And stare at each other.

Dogs. Barking. And howling.

"Oh my God! They're hunting us down!" Ava cries, and she runs up to stand next to me, scanning the dark woods around us.

The barking gets louder and louder, which can only mean one thing. "They're getting closer," I whisper.

"What should we do?" Ava asks.

"Run!"

I take her hand and we start cutting through the woods, heading away from the sound of the horrible howling and barking. The wind picks up and the trees raise their arms. They rattle their leaves angrily at us as we try to get away. I look sideways at them. The pines shiver and shake their leaves forcefully.

Pinecones start falling all around me. One of them pelts me on the forehead. Another one hits Ava's shoulder. I stumble and almost fall over a large root system that's twisted upward, protruding out of the ground.

The howling and barking continues to follow us. We stop and glance back for a moment. "What's that?" Ava asks, looking at the small light that seems to be following us.

I watch the light for a moment. It moves up and down and side to side, shifting directions in no particular pattern. "I have no idea," I tell her. "But I don't want to find out. Come on."

I find a twisted old tree. The trunk leans over to the left and I start climbing it. When I am standing on the first branch, I straddle it and lean over to reach down for Ava. "Come on. You can do it," I say, holding my hand out for her.

"I don't know," Ava hollers. "That's too high up for me."

The howling and barking gets louder and louder, and I reach for my little sister again, extending my hand as far down as it will go.

"You want to get away from the *Hounds from Hell*, don't you?" I ask her.

"The Hounds from . . ." Ava looks back. The barking is

getting louder and the light is coming closer. "Uh-uh, those are just regular dogs."

"The Founding Families are in control of everything! Anything is possible!" I whisper. "Come on! I don't want to get eaten alive by those hairy things!"

"Hey!" a low, raspy voice hollers. "Devil dogs! Get back here now!"

The gravelly voice sets Ava into motion, and she starts to climb the tree quickly. Once she's reached me, I have her follow me closely as we climb higher and higher, until we are a safe distance from the ground. Ava anchors herself on a branch and hugs the tree trunk while I stand beside her, holding on to a nearby branch to keep my balance.

"Just be quiet, okay?" I try to reassure her. "They can't see us. We're too high up."

Despite all my reassurances, and Ava's cooperation, it doesn't take the dogs long to find us. Within minutes, the beasts run right up to the tree and bark and whimper and holler like they've got rabies.

Ava closes her eyes tight and presses herself against the tree. She is shivering so hard, I'm afraid she might fall if she can't stop shaking.

"It's okay we're safe here . . ." I try my best to soothe my sister, but Ava is too scared, and she can't help but whimper and sniffle. I don't tell her, but I'm shaking, and my knees feel too weak to hold me up.

"Here?" the low, raspy voice asks. "What is it, boy? What do you see?"

"Is that . . . ," Ava whispers, so that only I can hear her. "Mr. Morris?"

I nod, but then I put my finger on my lips. "Shhhh . . . I think so."

"What's he doing . . . ?" Ava starts.

"Do you really want to know?" I ask her quietly.

Ava's eyes widen and she shakes her head quickly. I wipe her tears from her cheeks.

Under the tree, Mr. Morris continues to talk as he chases Peanut Butter and Jelly, trying to get them to settle down. "Where? Where? Show me where, boy!"

Then, the most unexpected thing happens. Peanut Butter and Jelly start to run up the bent trunk. Their huge long legs wobble and shake as they attempt to stay balanced on the tree, but they're doing it. They're climbing up here.

"What? Is someone up there?" Mr. Morris points his flashlight up into the tree and shines it directly into our eyes. "James? Ava?"

Mr. Morris sounds so worried about us—I just don't know what to make of him. I mean, *is he a good guy or a bad guy*? I can't tell, but the possibility that he might be working with the Martins, or worse, that he might be the Keeper himself, well, it frightens me. I can feel my weak legs melting under me. So, I hold on tighter.

"Is that you up there?" Mr. Morris asks when we don't say anything.

"Yes," I finally say, because it's not like we can pretend he can't see us.

The moment I answer, Peanut Butter and Jelly start wagging their tails. The friendly movements mess with their balance and they lose their footing. They fall gracefully, leaping off the tree and landing on their feet with two great big thuds. They shake off the fall and run around the trunk of the tree in circles, leaping and yelping like they just won a medal.

"It's late. What are you two doing up there?" Mr. Morris says, still holding the flashlight to look at us up in the tree. "I thought I told you two to stay out of the woods."

"Oh, we were just playing hide-and-seek," I tell him. "But then, well, we kinda got carried away."

"You have to go home," Mr. Morris says. "Strange things are afoot. You can't be out here! Not tonight! Come on. You can help me walk Peanut Butter and Jelly back to the house."

Peanut Butter and Jelly stop and yelp up at us when they hear their names. Mr. Morris leans down and grabs their leashes.

"What do you mean 'strange things are afoot'?" Ava asks.

"Haven't you heard? There's a full moon tonight," Mr. Morris says, tugging on the leashes to show Peanut Butter and Jelly that they're under his control again. The dogs yelp, lick their chops, and leap in place as they look up at us.

"So?" Ava asks.

"So . . . people and animals behave different . . . The full moon affects them in strange ways . . . Trust me, the woods are not safe tonight."

227

The Blood Moon is approaching.

The forest is about to come to life.

The words from the Keeper's letter come into my memory. My legs start to shake, and I push against the fear.

"Then why are you out here?" I ask him.

I am pretty high up, but even from this far up in the tree, I see Mr. Morris's shoulders droop as he looks down at Peanut Butter and Jelly circling around and finally settling at his feet.

He doesn't say anything for a while, and we sit together in that silence, Ava, me, Mr. Morris, and the forest. Until, finally, Mr. Morris stares out into the darkness and starts to speak.

"I lost my son during a full moon." His voice is quiet, solemn. "Twenty-five years ago. When we first moved here. He didn't like it here. Said these woods gave him nightmares. He said he sensed evilness out in that old cemetery."

At the mention of the cemetery, I slip quietly down a couple of branches. I want to make sure I hear this. Because I can sense it too.

"Evilness? Did he ever see anything?" I ask Mr. Morris. "Out there, in the cemetery."

Mr. Morris takes a deep breath and lets it out in a long, pained sigh that makes his whole body shiver. "I don't know," he says, shaking his head. "He went out there that night. Left us a note. And . . . and . . . we never saw him again."

"I'm sorry," I say as I take Ava's hand.

"I'm sorry too," Ava says. "Betty said she had a brother, but . . . she didn't tell us what happened. I'm sure it broke her heart."

"It broke everyone's heart," Mr. Morris says.

"This wasn't in any of the articles I printed," Ava whispers, and she starts to move down to the lower branch with me. "I guess I missed that one."

Some things about Mr. Morris's story ring true. And I want to believe him—I want to believe he's a really good person. But then, other things don't make sense.

"So, why are you still here?" I ask as we stand on a lower branch, close enough to the ground that I can see his face better. "I mean, why did you stay, if you think this place is dangerous?"

Mr. Morris takes a deep breath and sighs. Peanut Butter and Jelly creep up to him. They sniff his hand and whine quietly. "My wife wanted us to move," Mr. Morris says. "She was so mad when the community gave up and stopped searching for Seth. She wouldn't stop looking for him. But then the sheriff came around. Told her to stop investigating everyone and just let him do his job. And, well, she felt betrayed and didn't want to stay one more second in this *perfect* place."

"Is that your son's wagon?" Ava asks. "The one you use to pick up . . . things? When you walk around the neighborhood?"

"Yes. I made a promise after I lost our son. I swore on Seth's memory that I would patrol this strange place day and night. I promised him I'd watch everything and everyone. Never let these woods take even one more child from our community. Not as long as I live. Seth's wagon? Well, I feel like he's with me when I take it along."

"I can understand that," I say.

229

"So, what happened to your wife?" Ava asks. "Did she pass away?"

"She left," Mr. Morris admitted. "Just packed her things and took off in the middle of the night. Never will understand it. How she could just . . . walk away."

Mr. Morris's words make me shiver, because I remember another person, Ms. Phillips, who also *just left,* and I wonder if what he believes is true. *Did his wife really leave him and their daughter? Or did the Keeper make her disappear too?* But neither of these is a fact, just a feeling I get in the pit of my stomach.

"Please come down," Mr. Morris insists. "Let me walk you home. I have nothing but good intentions toward you."

I look at the dark, silent sky above, but I still can't see any stars, much less a Blood Moon. The truth is, we're lost. And my phone is dead. We can't get out of the woods without following Mr. Morris home.

When I start to move down, Ava puts her hand on my arm. "James? What if he's one of them? You know, one of *the others*?"

"If he was, he would have already called for backup," I tell her. "I'm not one hundred percent sure, but I think he's telling the truth."

"So, you think . . ."

"We should get down," I tell her. "We can always run."

I hesitate to put my foot on the ground, and I look once again at Mr. Morris, making direct eye contact. "You'll understand if we keep our distance," I tell him as Ava and I stay together. "We don't know you all that well."

"I wouldn't expect anything less from you two," Mr. Morris says, and he steps back, waiting for us to get going.

"Come on, Ava," I tell my sister. "You can do it. I've got you."

"Thank you, James," Ava says. "I think I've had enough hide-and-seek for one night. The woods aren't much fun."

"Well, I don't want to scare you, but I've been seeing some strange goings-on out here the last few nights," Mr. Morris admits as he struggles to keep up with PB&J.

"What kind of things?" I ask, a little creeped out by his words. Breathing heavily, we climb an incline and walk steadily past the tall gnarled trees in a deep part of the woods.

"Bizarre, peculiar things," Mr. Morris says. "Entire flocks of black birds diving into the woods and not coming back out. Deer leaving the area in droves, just walking down the highway by the dozens. Squirrels abandoning their babies. I know it sounds crazy, but in all my years of patrolling these woods, I've never seen anything like it."

I'm about to ask Mr. Morris where he came from and when he moved here, to try to figure out if he is or is not part of the Founding Families, when I see lights peeking through the dense woods.

"Is that . . . ?" Ava asks as we break through the tree line and get our first glimpse of Pine Circle again.

"My house," Mr. Morris says, "is right near yours. You want me to escort you home?"

"No," I say, stepping away from him. "We're good. Come on, Ava. Race you home!"

"Be careful!" Mr. Morris yells after us.

When we get to our house, I reach for the knob. But before I go in, I look toward Mr. Morris's house and see him waving at us before stepping into his home.

I wave back.

We enter the kitchen, which is dark, but as we turn left, we see our mother standing in the hallway. She is all dressed up in a fancy black dress.

That's when I remember—my parents are going to the Faculty Gala tonight! This is my mother's "big night." A big deal. But my mother doesn't seem to care, because when she turns around and sees me standing there, her eyes change and she runs toward me.

"James! Ava!" she cries when we rush toward her. "¡Ay, gracias a Dios!"

We wrap our arms around her waist and hug her. She hugs us back and squeezes us tightly. So tight that I'm afraid my lungs might collapse.

"Mom!" Ava cries into her side. "It was awful! We were so scared!"

"Where were you?" my mother asks. Then she pulls back and looks at us like she doesn't know what to make of us.

"We were . . . in the woods," I start. "You're not going to believe this, but Mr. and Mrs. Martin are part of a secret society of witches."

"Yeah!" Ava wipes fresh tears away from her face. "They're in a coven."

"They practice black magic and work for the Keeper—and they were going to sacrifice me tonight," I tell her.

"They kidnapped us!" Ava exclaims. "Put us in a cage. It was hot down there. And we couldn't get out. It was horrible."

"Coven? Keeper? Kidnapped?" my mother asks. "What are you two talking about?"

I catch a glimpse of my father coming down the hall toward us. Like our mother, he is all dressed up to go out in his dark navy suit and gray cowboy boots.

"James?" he calls out to me. "What are you talking about?"

At that very moment, a uniformed officer steps out of the living room and walks over to stand beside my father. I look at his badge. Sheriff Ben Michaels.

"Kidnapped?" Sheriff Michaels asks. "By the Martins? I just came from there. That's not what they told me."

"What?" I ask him, detaching myself from my mother to talk to the sheriff.

Sheriff Michaels pulls a small notebook out of his shirt pocket and reads from it. "Well, according to Mr. and Mrs. Martin, at approximately five thirty this afternoon, the McNichols children, James and Ava, broke a window, entered their premises, and vandalized their basement."

"Broke a window?" Ava leaves our mother's arms and steps forward to defend herself. "We didn't break anything! They trapped us. James first. Me second. They put us in a cage! And

233

they burned my things—including all my evidence!"

"Well, they called 911," Sheriff Michaels says, and he flips a page on his little pad and reads some more. "Among other things, the McNichols children muddied an antique wingback chair, broke the latch on their dog kennel, and shattered a precious vase. Mrs. Martin was very upset about that. It was a family heirloom."

"That's not true," Ava cries. "We didn't do any of that!"

"Not like that, we didn't," I tell Sheriff Michaels. "That's not what happened."

My father sighs and puts his hand up to signal that I should listen. I can tell by the way he's looking at me, with his eyebrows all bunched up on his forehead, that he's thinking, trying to figure this thing out.

"I tell you what," Sheriff Michaels says, flipping to another page and readying his pen over the notebook. "Why don't you tell me your side of this story."

So we tell him everything that we know about what's about to happen and where. We show Sheriff Michaels the envelope I took from the Martins' house, and he figures out it's some kind of invitation, though it doesn't have a place, only the time and date are listed. When we finish answering his questions, he stops writing and puts his little pad and pen back in his pocket. Then he turns to my father and sighs.

"Listen," he says. "I'm not here to arrest anybody."

"What?" I ask. "You're not going to arrest them?"

Sheriff Michaels turns to me and my mother. She has her hands on my shoulders, because she's trying to keep me calm. "Folks, one thing you need to remember is that my job is to follow the evidence. And the only real evidence I have is a vandalized basement and two eyewitnesses. Nevertheless, I see your children are scared. It's obvious they've experienced something traumatic tonight. I'm not discounting that," Sheriff Michaels explains.

"They have eyewitnesses?" Ava asks. "Eyewitnesses for what?"

Sheriff Michaels nods. "As I told your parents before you got here, Mr. Brent and Mr. Harvey corroborated the Martins' story. They saw you two fleeing the Martins' house and running into the woods about twenty-five minutes ago. Now, that doesn't necessarily prove anything, other than you were there. I still have to investigate this, piece everything together, figure out what really happened. You understand?"

"We do." My father pinches the bridge of his nose for a moment before he opens his eyes and gives Sheriff Michaels his full attention again. "Thank you, for taking our children's testimony into consideration."

"So, what happens now?" my mother asks.

Sheriff Michaels takes a deep breath and blows it out through his mouth. "Well, I think for now, we'll file these reports, theirs and yours," he says. "And hope that we get to the bottom of this in the next few days."

"So that's it?" I ask. "You're not going to investigate their secret society? They're meeting tonight, somewhere in the woods. You have the invitation. Find out where they're going!"

"I will look into it. I promise you," Sheriff Michaels assures us. "I'm not taking any of this lightly. Mr. and Mrs. McNichols, I know this has been a difficult night for you two. So, please, keep your children at home for the rest of the evening. It's just safer that way. For everyone involved. Watch a movie together. Have some scones and tea."

My father shakes the sheriff's hand. "Oh, don't worry, Sheriff, we're not letting them out of our sight."

CHAPTER 20

After Sheriff Michaels leaves, I plug my phone into the charger on the counter at the breakfast bar. My mother takes off her shawl and hangs it up in the hall closet. She's about to pull off her shoes when the doorbell rings.

"I'll get it!" my father hollers, and he walks to the front door and looks through the peephole while he tugs and pulls on his fancy tie. "Oh, it's the Johnsons."

Stephanie's parents walk into the room, looking worried. Their eyebrows are knitted together on their foreheads and Mrs. Johnson's clasping her hands tightly together.

"We don't want to intrude," she says, looking toward my mother, "but we saw Sheriff Michaels's car out here and, well, we didn't know what to think."

"I hope you understand," Mr. Johnson explains. "We were just worried."

"Oh, no," my mother says. "You're not intruding. Please, come in."

"Is everything okay?" Mr. Johnson asks. "Is there anything we can do?"

"We were kidnapped!" Ava says.

"Kidnapped!" Mrs. Johnson cries out. "When? Where?"

My mother puts her arm around Ava's shoulder and pulls her close. "As you can imagine, we're all still in shock," she says. "It's been a long afternoon. But, please, do sit down."

"Kidnapped . . ." Mrs. Johnson shakes her head as she follows my mother into the living room and sits down on the love seat because Ava plops herself on the couch, next to Baxter. "I just can't . . . Why, that's horrible. Horrible. Who would do something like that?"

"The Martins," Ava says.

"The Martins!" Mr. Johnson looks shocked. "Why would they do such a thing?"

"I can't believe it," Mrs. Johnson says. "Mrs. Martin seems so sweet. She's always been a little quiet and reclusive. God knows it took everything I have to draw her out of her house somedays, to join our community activities, but she's always nice about it. Are you sure? I mean, maybe there's some other explanation . . ."

"Oh, there is no other explanation," I say. "We were kidnapped!"

"And they're not nice. They put us in a cage and kept us there for hours," Ava whispers.

Mr. Johnson frowns. "A cage?" he asks me. "Where? In their house?"

"Well, it was more like a kennel," I explain. "But, yes, in the basement."

Mrs. Johnson reaches for her husband's hand and clings to him. "If I'd known what kind of people they were, I would have never . . ."

"It's okay." My mother leans over and pats Mrs. Johnson's arm. "You had no way of knowing."

"Just goes to show you," Mr. Johnson tells my father. "You never really know who you're dealing with. You think you live in a good neighborhood, a safe neighborhood, and then something like this happens."

"This could have happened to any of us," Mr. Johnson whispers. "That's what makes it so . . . disturbing."

I think about the fact that I was almost sacrificed by a crazy couple because they believe they can control nature, and I start to shiver. "But we're all right now," I tell Stephanie's mother, because I don't want Ava to relive the horror all over again. "We're safe now. And Sheriff Michaels said he was going to investigate everything."

"I'm sorry," my mother says, touching her temple with her fingertips, like she's just now getting a headache. "Where are my manners? Would you like something to drink? Coffee? Tea? Is it too late for a soda?"

"Oh, gosh, please don't fuss over us," Mrs. Johnson says. And she leaves the couch to follow my mother into the kitchen. "Please, let me take care of it for you. You should sit down and relax."

My mother sits at my favorite stool at the counter while Mrs.

Johnson starts a pot of tea in the kitchen. I hear a familiar noise, a soft vibration, and my mother looks over at my phone on the counter.

She unplugs it and hands it to me when I walk up to her.

"You have a message," she whispers, and she reaches over and ruffles my hair. But that's not enough for her, because then she pulls my head over and kisses my forehead, one, two, three times. "I love you, lagartijo!" she whispers against my face.

"I love you too," I tell her and, because I'm really feeling it, I lean over and give her a smooch on the cheeks Her eyes and dimpled smile tell me that makes her super happy.

When I look at my phone, I see that I have a message on my Three Amigos thread. A wave of relief washes over me, and I feel weak again, but for a much better reason.

"I'll be in my room, okay?"

"Okay," my mother says, and I take off running up the stairs while my parents visit with the Johnsons.

In my room, I plug in my phone and start texting back and forth with Beto and Mike for a while. They are being goofs, giving me grief about not being there for their soccer games.

ME: so the first game's tonight huh
BETO: pre-season tournament
yeah, it's going down
MIKE: dude get over here
ME: so now you need me
MIKE: yeah. we need someone to hand out towels

BETO: harsh

ME: funny not funny

MIKE: just kidding

wish you were here

to help us sweep up

ME: me too

well gotta go

family night

MIKE: got it

has to be done

BETO: has to

familia comes first

ME: for sure

gn

I don't tell them about the kidnapping because that's not the kind of thing I think anyone should text about. Even saying it on a phone conversation would feel too weird. So, I decide it's best to tell them the next time I see them. Dad promised we'd go visit everyone in Texas on Thanksgiving, so I'll have a whole week to tell them all about our abduction.

After texting for a while, I find out that Ava's been an hormiguita again. She's been digging deep and pulling up all kinds of dirt, trying to figure out what's going down there in the woods tonight, because she comes rushing into my room, breathless.

"I know why those birds are out there," she says, showing me a printout of a map. "This place used to be a massive swamp. Those birds used to live here. Thousands and thousands of them."

"What?"

"Look right here," she says, and she hands me the printout. "It's a map of how big that pond used to be. It's contained now, because it doesn't rain enough to flood the valley anymore. But it used to be huge."

"A swamp," I say, looking at our entire village circled on the map. "Of course. It makes sense. The Founding Families made this their home, but it's the birds' natural habitat. And now that they're regaining their powers, the birds are trying to reclaim it."

"That's what the Martins were talking about!" Ava says. "Oh, James. What are we going to do?"

"We don't have to do anything," I tell her. "Sheriff Michaels said he'd take care of it."

"But they're going to come back for you," Ava whispers. "If they don't go through with this, Brentville could be history. They can't take that chance."

"What?" I ask. "That's a stretch, don't you think? I mean, there's lots of things they could do to prevent that. Couldn't they, like, plant more trees or something?"

Ava goes to my closet and pulls out my gym bag. "James! Don't you get it? This is what they do! Take and destroy—the environment, animals, people—they don't respect life. They're not going to change now," she says. "We have to get ready for them."

"They are not coming for me here," I say.

"Yes, they are," Ava insists. "They have to. You heard what Mr. Martin said. Their future depends on it."

The gravity of the situation hits me hard, and I step back and try to wrap my mind around what we could do, what we have to do, if I'm going to survive the night.

I reach into my pocket and take out the blue crystal I took from the Martins' shrine.

"You're right. And even if they don't come for me," I say, "they might come for this."

"Well, I'm not going to just sit around waiting for them to take you again!" Ava jumps up and runs to her room.

I follow and watch her rummage through her closet. She brings out a long, sturdy lasso our parents gave her on her eighth birthday, when she became fascinated with the San Antonio Rodeo. Then we go back to my room and she throws it in my bag, along with a fresh roll of duct tape she finds in the hall closet. Ava comes back from our mother's office with a small bottle of holy water she got at the Basílica de Santa María de Guadalupe in Mexico City last summer.

"Really, Ava?" I ask her when she gives it to me. "We're not dealing with vampires here."

"Yes, but you never know what's going to work," Ava says, so she takes it back and in the gym bag it goes. "These are strange times, James. Well? Are you just gonna stand there? Or are you gonna help me?"

I go through my closet carefully, wondering if there's

anything we could really do to stop the Founding Families if they wanted to take me. Would they try to harm my parents? Not when we have guests, I don't think. They'd probably wait until we were all asleep to try to break in.

I'd feel so much safer if they weren't using magic.

I dig out a ten-ball roman candle. I find the lighter that my father purchased when he bought the fireworks and test it. It works. Then I throw everything in my bag, and grab an old boomerang I find in a box at the bottom of my closet.

"Where did this come from?" I ask, holding the boomerang in front of Ava like it's some kind of mystery object.

"I found it," she says, taking the boomerang out of my hand.

"Found it where?" I ask.

Ava thinks about it for a second before letting me in on her little secret. "In the attic. Don't get mad at me," she says, grinning like a tlacuache, a wily old possum hiding in a garbage can. "I've only been up there twice."

"You're such a snoop!" I tell her. But I'm only teasing her, because I know what she's like. There was no way Ava was ever going to stay away from my secret attic door. "Oh, wait. Maybe there's something good we can use up there!"

Ava looks through our rooms for other things we might use to fight off the Founding Families, while I grab my desk chair and crawl up into the attic.

But when I go through the boxes up there, using my phone's flashlight to light my way, there is really nothing worth hauling down. I find an old Swiss Army knife and shove it in my pocket. I'm sorting through a box of rusty nails, worn wrenches, and dull saw blades when I hear a loud thud coming from somewhere downstairs.

"Ava?" I call out, but she doesn't answer.

And when I point my phone flashlight across the attic, I see that the little door has been closed. *Seriously?* I think to myself as I abandon the box of tools. But when I try to open it, I discover that the door is stuck and, no matter how much I push and shove, I can't open it.

I'm trapped. *Someone's locked me up here!* "Ava! This isn't funny! Let me out of here!" I call out, but she still does not answer.

My heart beats wildly in my chest, and my chest feels tight, like I can't breathe all of a sudden. I tell myself I'm just anxious, and I try to calm down as I scan the attic for another way out. But, even as I walk the length and width of the floor, I know there is no other access door to this part of the attic.

"Ava! Ava! Can you hear me? Please answer me, Ava," I scream again, louder than the last time.

As I bang on the door with my foot, I hear a door slam, and I run over to the little attic window and open it. I don't need my scope to make out the silhouettes of two dark figures hauling my sister away as they run off into the night.

The Johnsons!

Stephanie's parents are part of the Founding Families!

My mind reels, and I can feel my whole body shaking as I try to make sense of what is happening. *Where are my parents?*

Without thinking about my safety, I put my arms over my head and squeeze myself through the small attic window. When I pull my legs through, I creep down the roof's incline and use the tree outside my window to climb down and run around to the front of the house.

But when I throw open the front door and run into the living room, I find my parents doubled over, asleep, on the couch, a plate full of scone crumbs in front of them and empty teacups in their hands.

"Mom! Dad!" I cry out as I rush to them. "Wake up! Please! Ava's in trouble!"

I tap their cheeks and put my hands on their shoulders, give them each a good shake, but they just won't wake up. I look at the plate and cups, and Sheriff Michaels's last words to us come back to me. *Keep your children at home . . . Watch a movie together. Have some scones and tea.*

I take the cup out of my father's hand and sniff it.

Orange-blossom tea . . . Mrs. Martin!

I hear shrieking, loud birdcalls coming from the window. Suddenly, a big black bird hits the windowpane. Its black claws and black feathers scratch and scrape at the glass as the bird fights to stay in the air, before it falters and falls with a faint thud to the ground below.

Suddenly, the television turns on, all by itself. On the blank screen, a single word appears . . . *WILLINGLY* . . . The misty white letters tremble and shiver, until they are eclipsed by a bloodred moon that grows and grows and takes over the entire screen.

I shake my father again, but he just snores louder than he's ever snored before. There's no time to wait! No time to plan. No time to strategize.

There is only time to act.

So, I run upstairs, grab the gym bag, come back down, and run to the garage for my bike. Then I pedal out of the driveway, flying down the road like a giant bird of prey, an avenging tecolōtl, as Ita might call me if she could only see me now, all grown up and ready to fight to the death to protect my little sister.

CHAPTER 21

I ride out to the pond and leave my bike standing by the tree line. There's no way around it, so I plunge through the thicket. Using my scope, I wind my way through the trees. But even with the night vision setting on, it is hard to see. The full moon is no help in these dense woods, and I find myself tripping on jutting roots.

I stand on the edge of a small clearing and almost scream when the howling wind swings the gnarled fingers of a tree branch and it grazes my ear and cheek. But I whimper and jerk back instead.

Swiping at my cheek, I step out of the woods and look around, trying to get my bearings. That's when I see it. Deep in the woods, a fire sparks to life. Dropping the scope, I take off.

With my heartbeat pounding in my ears, I run straight toward the enemy's lair. Out of breath and with my muscles on fire, I break through foliage, scramble around tangled tree roots, and leap over low boulders, to finally reach the edge of the clearing. From behind a tree, I take in the scene in front of me. I can't see the Founding Families' faces because they are wearing long, hooded green cloaks that match the robe I saw in the Martins' house. Ava is sitting by herself, on the ground, off to the left of the camp. I'm not sure, because it's hard to see from this angle, but I think her hands are tied behind her.

From my place in the woods, I spot a white-gray lechuza sitting on a nearby branch. I can tell it's not a tecolōtl because she has no feathered tufts on her head and her face is heart-shaped. But there's something strange and eerie about this lechuza. Her gleaming golden eyes almost glow in the dark as she stares at me and hoots.

Uhooooooooogggrt! Uhoot-hoot-hoot-hoot-hoot-hoot-hoot!

Uhooooooooogggrt! Uhoot-hoot-hoot-hoot-hoot!

Uhooooooooogggrt! Uhoot-hoot-hoot-hoot!

The sound reminds me of my Ita's stories. How she used them to teach us how to survive in the world, and the sight of that lechuza comforts me. Because I know I can do this. My Ita was right, we don't need magic. Ava and I have the best magic of all—we have each other. Ava is clever and I am brave, and together we can do anything. All I have to do is save my sister. Once she's free, I know we can defeat the Founding Families together.

There are seven of them, working to clean the area around the tombstones and what looks like some kind of altar, a tiered pedestal that wasn't there when we were down here a few days ago. One of them tosses what looks like ashes over the poop and feathers and nesting materials all those birds scattered around the cemetery. Two more sweep and scrub at the debris with brooms and rakes, picking it up and dumping it into the fire at the center of the camp. And all the while, the birds flutter and caw, caw, caw all around them.

Because I have to create a distraction, something that will buy me time to set Ava free, I climb a tree. From up here, I can see each of the members of the Founding Families clearly. Not only that, I can take good aim at them.

Quietly, I unzip my gym bag and reach into it to pull out the ten-ball roman candle. Praying that it's not a dud, I light it carefully and aim it directly at the circle of Founding Family members. The ten balls shoot out quickly, whizzing straight at each of the robed figures.

As each ball falls at the cult members' feet, their hems and long sleeves catch fire, and they begin to jump around, slapping themselves and trying to pull off their robes to stomp on them. The big black birds flutter away and circle around them, cawing and cackling. Three Founding Family members give in to their panic and run off, screaming, into the woods, still on fire! I wait for them to run past me before I scramble hurriedly down the tree.

With my scope swinging from my neck and my gym bag slapping against my thigh, I sprint toward my sister. My heart is racing, thrum, thrum, thrumming in my ears, but I tell myself it's fueling my body—making sure I can fight these people. Amid the chaos, I reach Ava and untie the rope to let her hands lose.

Ava throws her arms around me and says, "Thank you! Thank you!"

At that exact moment, a strong wind rushes into the clearing, chattering through the trees and sweeping up the leaves.

As debris swirls all around us, the four remaining members of the coven encircle us. As hard as we fight, they manage to hold us down and tie our hands behind us. No matter how much we struggle, we are no match for them.

I am sitting on the ground next to Ava, trying to figure out what to do next, when it happens. Out of the darkness, a shadowy figure appears. A strong wind lifts and curls the hem of their cloak as they walk toward us. They move so slowly, so smoothly, if I didn't know any better, I'd think they were floating and not walking into the camp.

All around us, the four figures move out of the way, mumbling and whispering.

"Keeper!"

"Keeper!"

"Welcome, Keeper of Life!"

"Welcome, Keeper of Homes!"

"Welcome, Keeper of Blessings!"

The members of the coven grovel as they drop to their knees and bow their heads.

"Rise, Order of the Blood Moon!" The Keeper commands them. Only it's not a man who speaks from under the hood but a woman. "Rise and let us call forth our Divine Friends!"

That voice! How do I know that voice? I ask myself as I struggle to free my hands from the thick ropes at my wrists. The Keeper's words go around and around in my mind. *Rise, Order of the Blood Moon! Let us call forth our divine friends . . . Rise! Order of the Blood Moon! Divine Friends!* But no matter how much I try to remember where I've heard that voice before, I can't quite place it.

"Who is she?" Ava asks quietly into my ear, and I shake my head.

Mrs. Martin's lip quivers as she lifts her eyes to the Keeper. "Forgive us, Master. But we only have three of the elemental stones."

"The *youngblood* has the stone," the Keeper says. Then, throwing back her hood as she turns to look at me, the Keeper asks, "Don't you, James?"

Ava gasps. "Mrs. Benson!"

"Wait?" I ask her. "It was you? All this time?"

Mrs. Benson smiles a strange, eerie smile as she starts walking toward us. "Of course," she says. "Who else would welcome you into the community so eagerly?"

"I don't understand," I tell her. "Out of all the children in the world . . . why me?"

"You are—exceptional," Mrs. Benson says. "The sacred stones

revealed your name to me years ago. I've been watching you for a very long time, but I had to bring you here for the tests."

"No!" Ava yells, struggling to free herself. "You can't kill him! I won't let you!"

As the members of the Order tighten their circle around us, Mrs. Benson lifts her arms high up in the air and speaks.

"Rise, Earth! Rise, Water! Rise, Air! Rise, Flame!" she chants. "Rise, Divine Friends! Rise and lend us your powers! Return to our humble embrace!"

Led by Mrs. Benson, the Order of the Blood Moon raises up their arms too. As they all chant and pray in a sort of trance, three of the members of the coven hold a crystal in their hands. The red, yellow, and green stones spin and whirl inches above their palms!

As I watch, a red flame begins to form. It wavers over the red crystal. Then a tiny golden tornado glimmers and swirls over the yellow crystal while a series of thin, tender brown roots grow out of a tiny, dark mound of soil over the green crystal. In my pocket, the blue crystal stirs and rustles. Its coldness penetrates through to my skin, and that's when I remember the Swiss Army knife.

Because they look like they're all in some kind of trance, I lean over to Ava. "Can you reach into my pocket?" I whisper. "I have a pocketknife."

Ava scoots. She leans sideways so that her little hands are able to pull out the knife and together we open it without too much of a struggle. "Don't move," I tell her as I saw through the rope at her wrists. "Just sit there, pretend you're still tied, and cut me loose."

She's almost done when the red, yellow, and green crystals stop spinning and the members of the Order stop chanting. Three of them close their hands around the crystals. They leave the circle and approach the tiered pedestal. Calmly, they insert the crystals into it. The stones burn brightly as they burrow into the pedestal's grooved cavities. With the ropes off our wrists, Ava and I sit up, because the Martins, Mr. Benson, and Mr. Harvey are once again forming a menacing circle around us. Their hoods are thrown back, revealing their faces. As they move in, I reach over and unzip my backpack on the ground.

"You know what to do," I say, and Ava nods.

As Ava reaches into the bag and grabs the boomerang, Mr. Benson and Mr. Harvey grab me by the arms and try to haul me up. But I resist, kicking and shoving at them, making it as hard as possible for them to lift me up and drag me away from my sister.

"Watch out!" I scream, but I am too late.

Mrs. Martin yanks the boomerang out of Ava's hands and turns around to throw it as far as she can fling it. She sends it flying through the woods, where it crashes through leaf and limb. But because of its nature, the boomerang comes back. It flies right at Mrs. Martin's face, hitting her on the forehead and knocking her out cold.

Picking up the boomerang, Ava runs and whacks Mr. Harvey

in the back of the head with it, so that I am free to struggle against Mr. Benson's grip. Mr. Harvey falls forward with a thud and lands unconscious on the ground beside me.

"Oh, come on!" Mr. Martin yells as he grabs my free arm.

He is strong, stronger than I imagined he would be, but I won't be contained. As Ava picks up a burning piece of firewood and chases Mr. Benson into the woods with it, I push myself off the ground and swing my legs up, half somersaulting in the air, and wrenching myself free of Mr. Martin.

"Augh!" I let out a great big grunt as I land on my feet, turn around, and rush Mr. Martin, tackling him to the ground.

Mr. Martin hits his shoulder against a sturdy gravestone, and he yelps as he clutches his shoulder. "My collarbone!" he screams. "He's broken my collarbone!"

I turn around and look for my sister. Having finished duct taping Mr. Harvey's hands and feet, Ava moves over and starts to tape Mr. Martin's feet. I am about to give her the thumbs-up when Mrs. Benson lifts her arms high up in the air and says,

"Air and wind, lift this child from off his feet!
Up, up, up, bring him forth into my keep!"

Because nothing happens, I turn left and take off, sprinting over graves and grassy mounds and jutting rocks to get away from Mrs. Benson, who starts chasing me. Suddenly, she appears before me, arms up, ready to capture me. I duck under her outstretched arms and hit the back of her knees with a broken branch, a move that brings her to her knees, crying and hollering, "You little jerk! I'll roast you twice for this!"

"¡Ándale!" I scream back to Ava as I step away from Mrs. Benson, who appears to have very little magical power left after using it all up to catch up to me.

Ava has finished taping Mr. Martin's hands and feet but is now squaring off with Mrs. Martin, who has awakened and is trying to grab her.

"Get her!" Mrs. Benson screams at Mrs. Martin as she starts limping toward me.

"Stop!" I tell Mrs. Benson. And I lift the broken branch high up in the air and threaten her with it. "I don't want to hurt you, but I will if I have to."

Mrs. Benson flies at me, but I run around her and push Mrs. Martin out of the way, so she can't get to my sister. As Ava and I leap and run around gravestones, I almost fall over when my foot hits a rut on the ground. I feel my ankle twist, but not enough to sprain or break it.

I recover quickly, but not quickly enough to get away from Mrs. Benson, who grabs me and puts me in a bear hug that goes around my shoulders and chest like a vise. I struggle and she tightens her grip.

"Where is the crystal?" she asks as she pulls me up, so that my feet are off the ground and I can't use that *push off and somersault trick* I used before.

"It's gone," I say, thrashing and kicking my legs around to try and free myself from her grasp. "You'll never use them again!"

"He's lying," Mrs. Martin says, holding Ava's thin arm in a sturdy grip before her. "The other crystals are vibrating. The Water Crystal is here. Where is it? Do you have it?" she asks as she gives my sister a good shake.

"I did," Ava says, turning her face up so that she can make eye contact with Mrs. Martin. "But I crushed it with a hammer."

I laugh.

"It's true!" I tell her. "You want to see the pieces? They're over there. In my bag. Let me go, and I'll show them to you."

"Liar!" Mrs. Benson tightens her grip on me. I can feel her powers leaving her. She's not as strong as when she first grabbed me.

"Murderer!" I yell back, and I pull my leg up and kick her shin as hard as I can.

"Augh!" Mrs. Benson screams, and her grip weakens.

I struggle and free my right arm and elbow her in the stomach. More angry than hurt, Mrs. Benson takes a deep breath and chants something under her breath. Calling upon the last of her powers, she tosses me across the camp like a rag doll, sending me flying several feet away from her.

I fall to the ground, at the foot of the altar. The force of my body slams against the tiered pedestal. The structure shakes, and the red, yellow, and green crystals fall to the ground beside me.

Ava kicks Mrs. Martin's shin and rushes to me. When she kneels down to check on me, the ground begins to shake. A great gust of wind rushes into the clearing, and all around us leaves and grass, bushes and trees, even the pedestal begins to shake and shiver. Then, lightning strikes, thunder rolls, and giant drops of rain start pounding down on us. They feel like hail more than raindrops.

"Oh, no!" Mrs. Martin cries. "It's happening. The elements are turning against us. Keeper of Homes! Keeper of Blessings! Please, tell us what to do! We can't let this happen."

Ava curls up beside me as the red, yellow, and green crystals begin to levitate, rising inches above the shaking ground, as if they are waiting for Ava and me to do something with them.

"The blue crystal," I whisper to my sister. "It's going crazy in my pocket."

"Whatever you do, don't let her have it," Ava says. I put my hand over my jeans pocket and press down hard.

"It's ice cold," I tell her. "I might get frostbite if we don't take it out."

As if mesmerized by the sight of the activated crystals, the Keeper and Mrs. Martin lift their arms and start to move in on us. As the red, yellow, and green crystals float and vibrate before us, the rest of the members of the Order of the Blood Moon start to creep out of the woods.

"They're back," I say. "Look at them. They're like zombies!"

"What are we going to do?" Ava scoots around so that she is clinging to my back.

"I don't know," I say. "But this thing is about to fly out of my pocket!"

Mr. Brent and Mr. and Mrs. Johnson come forward in their half-burnt robes, hoods half covering their heads, their faces fully exposed. They stand behind Mrs. Benson and Mrs. Martin, bemused by the sight of the crystals dancing in front of us all.

"He has it," Mrs. Martin tells Mrs. Benson. "The *youngblood* has the crystal."

"Give it to me, child." Mrs. Benson reaches her hand out toward me.

She tries to get closer, but the force of the vibrating crystals pushes her back, and she grunts and retreats. She stands before us, grimacing and holding her arm against her chest.

"I can't get it," Mrs. Benson tells the members of the Order. "The crystals are protecting him."

Mrs. Martin shakes her head. "We can't give up," she says. "Time is running out. The Blood Moon is approaching."

I look up at the sky above. The storm clouds move aside, and the full moon comes into view. It shimmers and shines like a golden orb in the dark sky.

Mrs. Johnson leans over to Mrs. Benson. "We must find a way of putting the crystals back into place."

I reach down, pick up a large rock, and nod at Ava.

Beside me, Ava picks up another big rock. Then I reach into my pocket and pull out the vibrating blue crystal. With a trembling hand, Ava plucks the yellow crystal out of the air. She clutches it tightly in her little fist.

"What are you doing?" Mrs. Benson cries, her voice quivering.

"Don't. Please. Please, don't do that!"

Ava and I fight the vibrating force of the crystals and press them against the ground before we bring down the rocks and smash the vibrating stones. The blue and yellow crystals crack. At the same time, the red and green crystals stop moving and fall to the ground with a stony thud. They roll to a stop among the crushed pieces of crystal between me and Ava.

"Nooooo!" Mrs. Benson screams.

"No!"

"Why? Why?"

Mr. Brent and the Johnsons moan and wail as they fall to their knees and watch me and my sister strike and destroy the red and green crystal too. The stones lose their glow, split, and crumble into several small pieces. Ava and I strike at the broken pieces of crystal at the same time that the wind stops blowing and the rain stops falling.

As Mr. Brent and the Johnsons wail, every ounce of energy leaves their bodies, and they fall sideways onto the ground and curl up like cochinillas.

"Stop!" Mrs. Benson wails as she falls down and crawls over to reach for the crushed crystals. "Stop! Please!"

Ava scrambles up and runs to where we left my gym bag. She takes the thick rope out of my bag and lassos Mrs. Benson, tightening the rope hard around her arms and torso and pulling it until she falls back, defeated. Then, because the Keeper has rolled over in pain, Ava takes the duct tape off her forearm and tapes together Mrs. Benson's hands and feet.

As I pound down on the crystal pieces, turning them into dust, Mrs. Martin falls forward and claws weakly at me, trying to take the offending rock away from me. "Help me, Robert!" she cries out, looking back toward her husband, who is still lying on the ground. "Do something, please!"

"What do you want me to do?" Mr. Martin calls back to her. "Can't you see I'm hurt?"

As Ava tapes up the rest of the fallen members of the coven, I bring down the rock and pulverize the last bits of crystal. On the ground before me, Mrs. Benson struggles against the lasso and tape, but she is too weak now. She can't do anything but lie on her side, wheezing for air.

I throw the rock aside and the members of the coven stare up at me from the ground, too stunned and too shaken to do anything but weep for what's left of the crystals, bits and pieces of glistening rainbow rivulets that soak into the ground.

"It's over," I tell Ava, who is holding above her the boomerang she retrieved from the ground, like she's ready to take someone down with it.

"Are you sure?" she asks.

I stand up and take the boomerang out of her hands. "I think so. I hope so."

"So, we did it," Ava says, grinning at me. "We defeated the Keeper and the Founding Families together!"

"We did," I say, and I put my arms around her and give her

a big hug because I know I couldn't have done this without her.

Then we stop, look at each other, and listen. From somewhere in the woods, a great yelping and hollering is coming toward us. The sound grows louder and louder, and we turn around and around, trying to figure out where it's coming from. Before we know it, Peanut Butter and Jelly come crashing through the woods, dragging a breathless human behind them.

"Mr. Morris!" I cry out because I am surprised to see him.

"Ava! James! Are you okay? What's going on?" Mr. Morris asks. He holds his chest and tries to catch his breath as he looks at the members of the Founding Families lying prone all around us.

Released, Peanut Butter and Jelly run over to Mrs. Benson and Mrs. Martin and growl and snarl and stand watch over them, making sure they don't get up and start giving us any more trouble. The members of the coven hide their faces within the folds of their burnt cloaks and weep and cough and wheeze.

"Yes, we're okay," Ava says. "What about you?"

Mr. Morris nods and takes a deep breath. "Yes," he says. "Yes. I just . . . ran a little too fast. I'll be fine in a minute."

On the ground, the members of the Order gasp for breath. They look like they've aged quite a bit since they collapsed and curled up on the ground like dried maple leaves.

"What's wrong with them?" Mr. Morris asks, and I look down at the moaning members of the Founding Families.

"They're part of a coven," I tell him.

Ava holds on to Mr. Morris's arm, to make sure he doesn't

pass out and fall. "They were going to kill James," she says. "But we destroyed their magic crystals before they could sacrifice him to the Blood Moon."

"A coven?" Mr. Morris's eyes narrow and his nostrils flare. He doesn't say anything, but I know what he's thinking. "So, they're dying."

"No. They're just weak," I say. "They're losing their powers."

Mr. Morris walks around looking at the members of the Order all coiled up like snakes shedding their skins. "Good riddance," he says.

"We should call 911," Ava says.

I pull out my phone and turn it on, but no matter how much I lift it over my head and point it in different directions, I can't get a signal. My phone is useless.

"Help us," Mrs. Benson wheezes. "Please."

"What can we do? This thing's not working," I say as I smack my phone against the palm of my hand, hoping against hope that I can get a signal.

"We leave them," Mr. Morris says. "To go get help."

As I continue to smack the phone around, Ava tugs at my shirt. I look up and see two sets of lights in the distance before I hear the engines roaring toward us. "What's that?"

"Vehicles," I tell her. "Two of them."

"Yes," Mr. Morris says. "An SUV of some kind, or a truck, and a car."

"SUV?" Ava's eyes widen. "Mom and Dad!" she squeals, and

263

she picks up my bag and starts running toward the lights flashing through the dense woods.

"Ava! Wait!" I yell, but she is not listening anymore.

"Go on. Go after her," Mr. Morris says. "We'll stay here with these monsters."

I shove my phone into my pocket and run after my sister. The lights get bigger and bigger, until they stop on the other side of the tree line. I hear a car door slam and then my father calls out.

"Ava! James!" he yells. "¡Jaimito! Ava!"

"It's them!" Ava screams back at me.

"Dad! We're over here!" I cry out, catching up to Ava and running beside her.

"Daddy!" Ava screams. "Daddy!"

As we run out of the woods, we see my father's SUV sitting in front of us with the lights still on and the driver's door wide open. Our father, standing thirty yards away with Baxter at his side, turns to look at us, and his shoulders suddenly slump forward because he is so relieved.

Baxter barks and starts to leap toward us.

"Oh my Lord," my father cries as he runs our way. "You're okay!"

"Yes," I say. "We're okay."

As my father embraces us, takes us into his arms, Baxter bounces around, barking and yelping with joy. A second vehicle appears. It comes to a screeching halt next to my father's SUV. I cling to my father's neck and watch my mother open her car door and scamper to us on wobbly legs because she is so happy to see us, she can hardly walk.

My father opens his arm for her, and my mother drops to one knee and embraces us. There are warm, wet tears on her cheeks as she kisses us over and over again. "¡Ay, gracias a Dios!" she keeps saying. "¡Gracias a Dios!"

"Are you okay?" my father asks. "Please tell me you're okay."

"Yes," Ava tells my father, while Baxter tries to lick her face off. "Yes. We're okay."

"We worked together," I tell my parents. "Like Ita said, and we defeated them! We defeated the brujas and brujos!"

"We woke up . . . and we couldn't find you," my father says. "We were so . . . scared."

"We've never felt so helpless." My mother shakes her head and starts crying all over again. "I'm sorry we weren't there for you," she wails.

"We're fine," I say. "We took care of each other."

"Who did this?" my father asks. "Was it the Johnsons? Or the Martins?"

"Yes. And the Keeper, Mrs. Benson," Ava says. "She's in charge of the Order of the Blood Moon, the Founding Families."

"Mrs. Benson?" my mother gasps.

In the distance, we hear sirens. "The police?" I ask.

"Yes," my mother says. "I was on the phone with them when I saw you all. They're coming. They know exactly where we are."

"They'll need several ambulances," I say. "The coven is in pretty bad shape."

"Several?" my father asks as he dials 911.

Ava nods.

"We don't want them to die," I tell her. "Nobody deserves that."

CHAPTER 22

Saturday morning, Ava and I sit on the steps of the back porch, staring at the dark woods, having chocolate de olla with our mother, because Oregon gets chilly when it rains. As I let the warm, cinnamon-sweet goodness of my Mexican cocoa slide down my throat, I can't help but feel bad.

The news about Mrs. Benson and the Founding Families has been rolling on every television channel for days. On the big screen in our living room, reporters said that every member of the Founding Families has been arrested for kidnapping after being hospitalized for dehydration and other illnesses they didn't even know they had. Doctors say this was because of their "traumatic experience" during what they think was an "unexpected tornado" that tore up their camp while they practiced "occult activities" in the woods.

Now that we are safe and sound, my father comes out of the house and joins us on the back porch. "Well, that was another network on the phone, wanting to see if we'll all go on the air and tell our story," he says. He pulls up slightly on the legs of his pants and sits down on the top porch step beside me. "I told them no, thank you. We don't need to relive that nightmare."

"Have some chocolate." My mother hands him his mug. "It's still warm."

In my pocket, my phone vibrates.

I pull it out and look up at my father. "It's Jack."

My father smiles, but then his eyebrows furrow and he looks a bit tense. He probably isn't thrilled that the son of one of the people who tried to sacrifice me is texting, but he doesn't say anything. Instead, he takes a sip of his chocolate and scans the horizon, where the dark tree line meets the bright sky.

JACK: Hey, James. It's me, Jack.

ME: what's up

JACK: Just checking in.

How are you and Ava doing?

ME: we're good

JACK: Cool. I wanted to say

I'm sorry about what happened.

ME: thanks

JACK: I hope you know

I had nothing to do with that.

Stephanie, Beth, and I, we didn't know.

ME: I get it

how are you

I mean . . . are you okay?

JACK: Yeah. I'm staying with my aunt for now.

ME: good

JACK: So, are we okay?

I think about this for a moment. It's not Jack's fault that his parents were part of some dark occult group. Just like it's not Stephanie's or Beth's fault that their parents were willing to sacrifice a child for the sake of their families because they were that scared of losing their homes and their way of life. In a way, I feel bad for Jack. He's just a kid, like me and Ava. I mean, parents make mistakes, right?

ME: yeah we're okay

JACK: Cool beans.

I look up, and my father's peeking down at the phone in my hands. I lean it over so he can read the last few lines on the screen.

"Good man," my father says, and he reaches up and ruffles my hair.

From her chair on the porch, Ava rests her head on her arm and looks out at the piney woods beyond the tree line, where a flock of black birds is soaring. "School's about to start," she says. "I hope they teach us about the environment. I want to know everything there is to know about these trees and these birds. How to take care of them. How to protect them."

"I'm sure they'll teach you all about that," I say, setting my hot chocolate beside me on the porch floor.

My mother, who is sitting in her rocking chair on the edge of the porch behind me, leans over and wraps her arms around my shoulders and hugs me tight. She pushes my hair back, kisses the crown of my head, and says, "And what about you, James? What are you hoping to learn this year?"

I think about it.

There's only one thing that interests me. One thing that I don't know a lot about.

"The stars," I tell her. "I want to know more about what's out there. In the heavens. Waiting for us."

"Well, that sounds good. Maybe you'll work for NASA someday. Mission Control's in Houston, you know," my mother says. Then she lets me go and starts to get up. As she leans over, I notice the moonstone owl pendant hanging from its long silver chain around her neck.

"Is that Ita's necklace?" I ask, because I remember my Ita wearing it in my videos.

My mother puts her hand up to her chest and picks up the pendant to look at it.

"Yes." Her wide lips curl up into a dimpled smile and her amber eyes sparkle. "It sure is."

"Tecolōtl," Ava says. "Owl."

"Lechuza," my mother corrects. "A modern symbol of the Tlātlāhuihpochtin, a small reminder that we are all luminous creatures—that no matter what the darkness brings, we always have the choice to be a light in the world."

"Words to live by," my father says as he raises his cup of chocolate before our small family circle.

"Words to live by!"

My parents, Ava, and I clink our cups together, sip, and look up at the sky.

"It's going to be a glorious day," my mother whispers.

"Hmm." My father nods. "Let's hope this good weather stays with us for a while! Winter will be here before you know it, and I don't know exactly what that will look like."

"Whatever it is, we can handle it," I say, because the morning's rain is quiet and soft, and the sun is gleaming, golden and bright, through the blue-gray clouds as they pass us by.

ACKNOWLEDGMENTS

First and foremost, I want to thank our heavenly Father for all His blessings. I am humbled every day by His loving-kindness, for pulling me out of the darkness and shedding light on my life. I wouldn't be here but for His grace.

I also want to thank my husband, Jim, for being my beta reader, my first eyes, and helping me see the plot holes in all my stories as well as in life. You make this journey so much easier! To our sons, James (my Jaimito), Steven, and Jason, who continue to celebrate, honor, and support my creative endeavors by indulging me when I sit around telling them all about my latest book, thank you for listening!

A great big, giant thank you goes to my agent, Andrea Cascardi, for all the work she does out there in the world to support me. I am so grateful for your guidance, Andrea. Your generous heart keeps me hoping and dreaming, creating new stories for my community.

There are so many people to thank as I sit here in the lobby of the Hoover building at George Fox University in Newberg, Oregon. This community, this special campus, and my colleagues have all played a huge role in the development of this manuscript by supporting me in the best possible way. I am forever grateful to Dr. Gary Tandy, who, along with Dr. Melanie Mock and Dr. Bill Jolliff, brought me here to this wonderful, glorious place where I have found the peace and space to create. Thank you all for being so kind and compassionate with me, for sharing your time, for mentoring me, and for being such good friends. You have my corazón!

And to my friends in Texas, thank you for staying in touch and keeping up with my shenanigans out here in the PNW through social media. I love you and miss you very much!

You are all blessings in my life!

GLOSSARY

abuelita—grandmother

¡Águila!—Watch out!

¡Ándale!—Come on!

¡Ay, gracias a dios!—Oh, thank God!

antepasados—ancestors

brujas/brujos—witches /warlocks

cariño—beloved one

chisme—gossip

chismosas—gossipy or nosey (feminine)

chocolate de olla—a thick, cinnamon-flavored hot chocolate drink made in a pot on the stove, usually using dark, rich chocolate bars

chucho—pooch, doggie

churro—long, thin, crusty piece of pastry that is fried, drained, and then dusted with cinnamon and sugar

colcha—home-made quilt

como cochinilla—like a little pill bug

consejos—bits of advice, tips

cucarachas—cockroaches

cucuy—something to be afraid of; a boogeyman or a thing that goes bump in the night

cuentos—stories, tales

cuervos—large black birds of the crow family

familia—family

hasta luego—See you later

hermano—brother

hormiguita—little ant

ita—a diminutive of abuelita, short for granny

La Llorona—In folklore and myth, La Llorona, or Weeping Woman, is said to be the ghostly apparition of a woman who drowned her children in the river during a fit of jealousy. In regret, and as her eternal penance, La Llorona wanders the rivers and lakes of the world, looking for her children, calling out, "¡Ay, mis hijos!" in spine-chilling, haunting wails that echo through the darkness.

lagartijo—small house lizard

lechuza—A barn owl, identified and distinguished by the heart-shaped facial disk; elongated, compressed bill; small eyes; long legs; and dark plumage, which are very different from a regular or typical owl (tecolōtl). Also, in mythology, a Lechuza is said to be a woman who used to be a witch and upon death turned into a screeching witch owl, bringer of bad news, tormentor of souls, and harbinger of death.

mechas—wild, untamed hair locks

mi amor—my love

montes—woods

muñecas—dolls

Nahua—Indigenous population groups of Mexico, of which the Aztecs are known members

ofrenda—offering

ojitos—little eyes or loving eyes

pesadillas—nightmares

queso fresco—a mild, crumbly white cheese similar to feta or ricotta

rebozo—shawl

relampago—lightning

sana sana colita de rana. Si no sanas hoy, sanarás mañana—lyrics from a well-known Mexican nursery rhyme /folk song that translate to, "Heal, heal, little frog's tail. If you don't heal today, you'll heal tomorrow."

sonsa—foolish or simpleminded

susto—a good scare, fear

taquitos de res—beef street tacos

tecolōtl—a regular or typical owl, distinguished by its heart-shaped facial disk; large, elongated eyes; short hooked bill; thickly feathered legs; and mottled plumage. A bird of prey just like its cousin the Lechuza, or barn owl. The tecolōtl is featured prominently in several Nahua stories.

tiliches—slang for stuff, as in one's belongings

tlacuache—opossum

tlātlāhuihpochtin—In Nahua mythology, these people are followers of the sorceress Malīnalxōchitl, priestess of Quilaztli (a motherhood and fertility goddess). This group is also known as "the luminous" or "the luminous ones."

tortas—sandwiches made with personal-size French bread or ciabatta stuffed with cold or hot meat, cheese, and a wide selection of vegetables, like thinly sliced cabbage, iceberg lettuce, Roma tomatoes, jalapeños, etc., and smothered with salsa

¡Uy!—an expression to show a scared or creepy feeling, similar to "Oh!"